If a Tree Falls at Lunch Period

GENNIFER CHOLDENKO

If a Tree Falls at Lunch Period

Harcourt, Inc.
Orlando   Austin   New York
San Diego   London

www.HarcourtBooks.com

Library of Congress Cataloging-in-Publication Data
Choldenko, Gennifer, 1957–
If a tree falls at lunch period/Gennifer Choldenko.
p. cm.
Summary: Kirsten and Walk, seventh-graders at an elite private school,
alternate telling how race, wealth, weight, and other issues shape their
relationships as they and other misfits stand up to a mean but influential
classmate, even as they are uncovering a long-kept secret about themselves.
[1. Family problems—Fiction.   2. Race relations—Fiction.
3. Overweight persons—Fiction.   4. Social classes—Fiction.
5. Schools—Fiction.   6. Popularity—Fiction.]   I. Title.
PZ7.C446265If   2007
[Fic]—dc22   2006028664
ISBN 978-0-15-205753-4

Text set in Goudy Old Style MT
Designed by April Ward

First edition
A C E G H F D B

Printed in the United States of America

To my editor, Kathy Dawson, who reads between
the lines, between the letters, and even between
the dot on the *i* and the stroke itself
—G. C.

ONE

Kirsten

This is lame but I'm actually looking forward to school this year, because every day this summer was like crap: dog crap, cat crap—I even had a few elephant crap days. Trust me, it was bad.

For starters I hardly saw my best friend in the whole world, Rory. She was always in camp or on Maui.

They probably don't even have crap on Maui.

Besides Rory being gone all summer, my only other friend in the whole world, Nellie, moved away and my mom and dad fought all the time. They stopped seeing my little sister, Kippy, and me, and they definitely stopped hearing what we said. We even tried a little experiment on them. Kippy said there was a colony of worms living in the laundry hamper and my mom said: "Leave your muddy shoes outside." And I said Brad Pitt had invited me to a slumber party and my mom said: "You already had your snack."

It was funny for a while. Then it wasn't.

But summer is over. School is back. And all I can think about as my mom drives us up to the drop-off is how I really, really, really want to have a bunch of classes with Rory this year. Well, that's almost all I think of. I also consider my butt and how it will make its way out of our car. Nobody wants to see a gigantor butt coming out of a car first thing on a Monday morning, that much I know.

"Have a good day. Eat the lunch I packed. Don't buy junk . . . ," my mom says when my feet hit the pavement.

"Kirsten!" She unrolls the side window and beck-ons with her hand. "Do you know that boy, that bla— African American kid?" Her head cranes toward a guy who just got out of a red sports car. Tall, nice-looking guy. Shaved head, handsome . . . dresses like he's the governor's son.

I shrug. "Must be new."

The red car pulls out of the drop-off and my mom's head snaps to the front. She pounces on the accelera-tor and her car flies forward with the door open and the seat belt clanking the side. She swerves around a big SUV, guns it, then pounces on the brakes, coming to a squealing, screeching halt.

The stop sign.

Her hand rotates a million miles an hour, gesturing to this poor huddled pedestrian, but the pedestrian won't move. He's afraid. I can't blame the guy. . . . I'd be afraid, too.

When my mom sees the man is sticking, she shoots forward again like she's on the chase. She's hunting down the red car, going to drive right over it and staple it to the ground.

Oh, great: now she's getting weird in public, too.

When I turn to leave, the black kid is standing next to me. "That your mom?"

I nod, then giggle. God, I hate my giggle. You have to be size three and named Barbie for my giggle. Between my giggle and the extra forty pounds, I've got to be the coolest girl in the whole seventh grade.

"She hits my mom's car, gonna be trouble." He shakes his head. "You don't wanna mess with my mom and that car."

"I'm sorry." My face flames so hot I could fry eggs on my cheeks.

"That's a 350Z. We just got it. My mom's been shining it with her toothbrush. You should see her."

"It's nice." I bite my lip. "Very red."

"My mom drives it real careful. She has two speeds. One mile an hour"—he pauses—"and stopped."

I laugh—my real laugh this time.

"I thought the police were gonna pull us over for going so slow. Like, hey lady, get outta neutral." He shakes his head.

The warning bell rings. "We gotta move!" he says.

"You go. I'll never make it!"

"Come on, whatever your name is, *run*," he shouts over his shoulder.

3

"My name is Kirsten," I call after him as he thunders ahead taking the stairs two at a time.

I try running, even though running makes my fat jiggle. Still, I want to keep up. This guy is nice to me even though my mother nearly creamed a guy in the crosswalk and chased down his mom's car. My *mother* . . . I swear. What was that about, anyway?

TWO

Walk

"C'mon!" Walk yells back to the big white girl Kirsta? Kristal? Whatever her name is.

He races down the hall and kills the stairs. His feet are burning; doors, lockers, kids are flying by.

He knows where the class is because he and his momma, Sylvia, walked the schedule last week. He can't be late. Not on the first day.

The bell rings.

He's late.

Walk slides into an empty seat Matteo saved for him. Matteo is the only kid he knows here.

The girl is behind him breathing like somebody better dial 9-1-1.

The old guy up there with the belly and the long hair? Must be Balderis, the history teacher. The man's all red like a pimple—even his ears and his nose are red. He opens his mouth like he's going for the slaughter, then shuts it again, shakes his head, takes a deep breath, and starts over. "Your name is?"

Sweat pours down Walk's back. "Walker Jones."

"And yours?" Balderis looks at the girl.

"Kirsten McKenna."

"Mr. Jones," Balderis says, "would you and Ms. McKenna please see me at the back of the room. And the rest of you need to read chapter one of McDougal. I trust you all have brought your McDougal. I'll be giving a pop quiz at eight forty-five."

"What, is he *crazy*? This is the first day," a kid mutters.

"Just refuse to do it. If everyone does, then what'll he do?" another kid says.

Walk shoves past Matteo, who is already reading McDougal, scritchy-scritching the words all neon yellow. Matteo looks up. His smile spreads slowly across his face: he gets an extra five minutes to study—*the rat.*

Walk would have been on time, too, if he hadn't stuck around to talk to Kirsten and watch her mom lay rubber on the drop-off.

"You weren't in your seat when the bell rang, Walker. Kirsten, you weren't even in the room." Balderis crosses his arms; he taps his foot. "But . . . I'm going to call you both on time, seeing as how this is day number one and I need students to help me move my classroom to room 251 this Saturday. I will expect you both to be here at nine A.M.—or Monday you'll be marked tardy and sent to the office, should you be late or not. Am I making myself clear?"

Sylvia will destroy Walk if he messes up at this

school. Crush him to itty-bitty bits. If this Balderis guy wants him here dressed like a reindeer with a red nose, he'll say uh-huh. "Yes," Walk says.

"You want us here on *Saturday?*" Kirsten sticks her chin out. "I have to ask my mom."

"By all means ask away. Just remember, you don't show up for any reason and Monday you'll march into the office for a pink slip, understand?"

"Yeah, okay," Kirsten mumbles.

"Nine o'clock." Balderis taps his hand with his pencil. "I expect you to be on time Saturday, too."

"Hey," Kirsten whispers on their way back to their desks. "You're gonna give up your Saturday for one measly pinky?"

"You better believe it, girl," Walk says.

"Attention please." Balderis raises his voice now. "Anyone late to this class *for any reason* will be sent to the office for a trouble slip. Understood? In lieu of a pink slip Kirsten and Walker here have generously agreed to help me move our room on Saturday. That's available to you as recourse for a late slip, *this week only.*"

"We're moving?" asks a kid with so much hair, if it wasn't for his nose, you couldn't tell the back of his head from the front of his head.

"Someone puked in the heater vent," a girl in fatigues tells him.

"Someone puked in the heater vent, so we're *changing classrooms?*" Walk whispers to Matteo. "How

Walk

many classrooms they have here, anyway? Couldn't they just clean the vent?"

"Yeah, Burrito Boy . . . ," a hot blond girl tells Matteo, but Walk doesn't catch the rest of what she says. Whatever it was must have been bad, because Matteo's eyes go dead like he's climbed right out of his face.

"What?" Walk asks, but Matteo doesn't answer. His nostrils flare. He keeps his mouth closed.

After class Walk tries again. "What did that girl say to you?"

"What girl?"

"The blond sitting across from you."

"Nothing." Matteo zips up his organizer, with all the pencils pointing the same way.

"What's her name?"

"Brianna Hanna-Hines. Her dad made a billion bucks writing a book, *Women Are Toads. Men Are Toadstools.*"

"*Women Are Toads. Men Are Toadstools?*" Walk whispers.

"Uh-huh. And the auditorium is called the *Hanna-Hines* Performing Arts Building. Brianna *Hanna-Hines.* Starting to make sense to you?"

"Her parents are loaded. But what she say to you make you look so . . ."

"Make me look so what?" Matteo glares at Walk.

"Like . . ." Walk sucks in his breath. "Never mind, man. Never mind."

8

THREE

Kirsten

O h my god, *I can't believe it. I only have one measly little history class with Rory, plus I came in late and there weren't any seats near her.*

"You could have saved me a seat," I mouth.

Rory's face scrunches up like she can't read my lips.

At least we have the same lunch. Of course, everyone in the whole seventh grade has the same lunch. Soon I'm going to be happy to have feet in my shoes and snot in my nose, too.

When the lunch bell rings, I head straight for where Rory and Nellie and I used to sit. But Rory isn't there. Where is she?

Half of lunch is over before I finally track her down standing in line to sign up for the talent show auditions. Wow, they're starting early this year. "Are you going to be rehearsing for the talent show *at lunch?*" I ask.

"I dunno." She runs her fingers through her hair. "But know what I heard? They're going to have a real director and a makeup artist and a costume designer. I mean real famous people. You gotta sign up. You do."

"I can't. I have no talent. Unless keeping the tops on my gel pens counts."

"No, really, you could, like, dance or something. C'mon. Kir, you have to."

"Hello? Take a look at my butt. Do you really think I should be wiggling it *in front of people?*"

"C'mon . . . guys check you out all the time."

"They used to. Now they just try to figure out how to get around me in the hall. Butt approaching on the left: steer right, steer right!"

"Your butt is not that big and you know it."

"Seriously, you haven't seen me in six weeks. Am I like a walking condominium now or what?"

Rory bites her lip. "You look great, Kirsten. I don't know what you're talking about."

"You're lying."

"Really, Kir, this talent show is like the most exciting thing that's ever happened to us! Ever! I heard the budget is twenty-five thousand dollars and we're going to have real costumes."

"Twenty-five thousand dollars for the talent show? *Our* talent show?"

Last year the high point of the talent show was when this weird kid named Hair Boy did barking seal imitations. Who would spend twenty-five thousand dollars on that?

I don't say this, though. I don't want to spoil her

fun even if rehearsal might cut into lunch period, which is practically the only time I get to see her. Besides, Rory actually does have talent. She can really sing.

I wait in line with her for the rest of lunch, sketching costume ideas for her.

Kirsten

FOUR

Walk

He met Matteo last January on his tryout day at Mountain School. They gave Walk a bunch of tests that day and he had to spend the afternoon in class. Apparently you can't just apply on paper. They have to meet your live body and make certain you aren't defective. The teacher assigned Walk a buddy like it was kindergarten. The buddy was Matteo.

Walk couldn't figure Matteo at first. His upper body was all pumped like whoa, watch out, but his hair was flattened down like he was six and his momma combed it for him. And the way he kept his binder so neat it looked like the surgical supply closet at the hospital where Sylvia works.

But the thing Walk really didn't like about Matteo was how he let them call him "Burrito Boy." "Why you let them do that?" Walk asked that first visit-the-school day.

Matteo shrugged. "I like burritos."

"They call me corn bread or collard greens, gonna be trouble."

Matteo laughed.

"I'ma call you Matteo, okay, man?" Walk said.

"Yeah, okay." Matteo nodded, but Walk couldn't tell what Matteo thought about this. It was hard to know what Matteo thought about anything that first day.

Right after Walk got the letter that said he got into Mountain, he got one from Matteo. It was Matteo's buddy job to make Walk feel the love, which was pretty lame, except then they ran into each other over the summer. Sylvia signed Walk up to tutor little kids in reading and math. She thought it would look good on his high school applications. All the other tutors were girls so Walk and Matteo hung out together a lot. They were friends now. Real friends.

Walk wishes Matteo were black instead of Mexican, though. He doesn't like being the only black kid in his grade—one of three at the whole school. It makes him feel like there's a giant bull's-eye painted on his naked brown booty.

By last period all Walk can think about is going home, and blasting his tunes so loud he can't hear his brain yakkity-yakking in his head anymore. He looks at the poster on the wall. It's a kid's drawing of people of all colors holding hands around the earth. ONE WORLD: CULTURAL DIVERSITY AT MOUNTAIN, it says.

Diversity . . . yeah, right. Everyone here is white. Is this place for real or what?

Walk

FIVE

Kirsten

In the kitchen after school, I head straight for the ice cream. We have two kinds: vanilla for Kippy and mix-in peanut-butter Snickers for my dad. When I pull the top off the mix-in Snickers, I recognize my signature spoon work.

"No more," I tell myself, grabbing some grapes. I walk by the hall mirror quick, without looking. I'm going to be thin soon, no point in looking at myself fat.

Only thing about fruit is I swear it makes me ravenous. The next thing I know, I'm walking back to the kitchen in a trance—the sugar is calling me: *Come to the Mother Sugar.*

I pick all the Snickers bits out. Now the ice cream looks like vanilla. Why stop now? Dr. Dad won't notice. Dr. Dad is busy, busy, busy.

Back in my room, I spread my geometry homework out on my bed and try hard on the first problem.

It doesn't make sense, so I switch on my computer to see if Rory has emailed me back.

YOU HAVE NO NEW EMAIL.

When was the last time she sent me an email? How come I always email *her* now?

Don't be silly, Kirsten, I tell myself. That is *so* elementary school. Best friends don't worry who was the last person to email. Besides I just had lunch with her. She wasn't mad. Not one bit.

I'm just about ready to send her another email when Kippy pounds down the hall. She sticks her head in my room with a wad of lettuce in her hand. "You want to feed the rabbits?"

I follow her downstairs. My mom is on the phone in the kitchen. Instantly, the ice cream goes radioactive in my stomach. She can see it in there, I know it. But luckily she's talking to someone from my school's auction committee. She just got voted to be something or other and she's very excited about it. Maybe she won't notice. I give her my most winning smile and follow Kippy down the steep basement stairs.

Kippy and I love our basement. For a while she was obsessed with getting bunk beds so we could live down here, but my mother wouldn't go for it. When we were younger we used to play flashlight tag in the basement for hours. I was always Krypton One and she was Krypton Two. Kippy likes chemicals. She's going to be

15

Kirsten

a chemist when she grows up, if she doesn't blow us all up first.

Plus Kippy has her favorite books here—all nonfiction stuff like *The True Story of Dirt*. She refuses to read anything that's "fake." I have a TV and an Exercycle my mother installed smack in front of it. My mother is subtle, isn't she?

With our rabbits, Mr. and Mrs. Bunn, munching happily on their dinner, Kippy heads for her chair and cracks open *The Wonderful World of Worms*. I move a chair over to the TV and click it on. Every day my mother takes the chair away. Every day I drag it back. Today I push the Exercycle so hard it nearly tips over.

"You okay, Krypton One?" Kippy asks over the sound of my channel surfing.

"I'm okay, Krypton Two."

Surprise, surprise, my dad is home tonight. I scoot into our breakfast nook, where we always eat dinner. The chairs in the dining room are white silk. Even my mother is afraid to sit on them.

"So," my father says, sawing his chicken very carefully, as if he is being judged on how straight he cuts, "how are my brilliant girls? Studying hard, I trust?"

"Yes, Daddy," Kip says.

"And you, Kirsten? How's the math going? Do you want some help?"

I shake my head fast. I'd rather flunk than make a

mistake in front of him. Drowning, smothering, and burning to death would be better, too.

"Tell your father to leave you alone," my mom says.

"Tell your mother I'm just asking," he tells me.

Here we go again. "Hey, guess what?" I say. "I'm going to school Saturday morning for . . . extra credit."

"Extra credit?" he asks hopefully.

"Okay, well, it isn't exactly extra credit. More like detention but, hey, that's close enough, isn't it?"

He opens his mouth to say something, but before he can, Kippy jumps in. "You didn't ask about second grade. We are doing an in-deep study of the letter *P*. *P* is very important. How could you spell psoriasis without a *p*? Jenna W. said everyone knows psoriasis starts with an *s*. And I said, excuse me but it starts with a *p*. I can spell all the McKenna diseases: Corns. C-o-r-n-s. Vaginitis. V-a-g—"

"No. Oh please. You didn't say that," my mother interrupts, her neck flushed.

Kippy nods, her little face dead serious.

"What did Mrs. Hamsterhead say?" I ask.

"Mrs. *Hamstall*." Kippy glares at me. "She said some words you only spell in private, but how's she going to know I can spell them if I only spell in private?"

"All right, Kippy, we get the idea," my mother says.

"Ask your mother how her day was," my father says to me.

Kirsten

My mother's eyes drop to her plate.

"Tell your father who we saw today," my mom says.

"Who did we see today?" I ask her.

"The new boy," my mom says.

"Mom, what was that all about, anyway? It almost seemed like you were trying to chase down his mom's car."

"I'm the new volunteer coordinator," my mom snaps.

"Yeah, so? His mom didn't volunteer for anything and now you have a warrant out for her arrest?"

My father laughs, a weird laugh like maybe he's choking.

"I just want to meet her is all," my mother says. She gets up from the table and grabs the plates. If you want to finish a meal at our house, you have to bolt your plate to the table or my mom will whisk it away.

"What's for dessert, you might be wondering? Anybody wondering?" she asks. "I've got some delicious kiwi for Kirsten and me. And I brought home a boysenberry pie for Kippy and . . ." My mother sticks two pieces of pie in the microwave.

"Tell your mother I've got my heart set on a bowl of Snickers ice cream," my father says.

All the blood drains out of my face. "You know, I think I'll have the kiwi later, Mom. I'm going to get cracking on my homework." I scooch in my father's direction hoping he'll get the hint and move out of my way.

My mom's eyes waver. A line appears between her eyebrows.

"Excuse me, Dad, could I get by?" I ask as politely as I can.

"Tell your father I got the pie fresh from the bakery. It will taste a lot better today than it will tomorrow." My mom presses at her temple with her thumb.

"Tell your mother I'd rather have my ice cream." My father points his spoon at me.

The microwave chirps. Kippy's lips start moving. She is probably reciting insect subgroups. She does this when they fight. My father stands up, and I get out of there as fast as I can.

"Tell your father *your sister* ate his ice cream," I hear my mother tell Kippy as I climb the stairs. "Tell him your sister has gained thirty pounds in the last six months. Tell him maybe he should ask himself why."

"You're going to blame me for *that?* Why not just blame me for global warming, too?"

"Oh yes, you're totally blameless . . ."

I shut the door of my room so I can't hear them anymore. Then I take all the clothes out of my dresser. I fold each piece and put it back in the drawer as neatly as I can.

I do this perfectly. Totally and completely perfectly.

SIX

Walk

"How did it go?" Sylvia asks. She takes the day off just so she can pick up Walk at 3:00 instead of at 5:30 like she usually does. Sylvia tries to pretend it's no big deal, but she never takes a day off for something like this. Never.

"Fine."

"Who did you meet?"

"Kids."

"And their names are?"

Walk frowns at her.

"But it went all right?" she asks.

"It went fine."

Sylvia sighs. She pulls into the 7-Eleven and hands Walk a five. "Get whatever you want."

Sylvia is handing him money for *junk food* . . . now that's unusual.

Soon as Walk enters the store, the guy comes out from behind the counter. He follows Walk down the aisle to the chips and stands making a lot of noise straightening the fruit pies while Walk picks out his snack. The guy's an idiot. Somebody could steal the whole cash register while he makes sure Walk doesn't stuff a pastry in his pocket.

He follows Walk to the cooler where he gets his Gatorade and then back to where Walk puts his stuff on the counter. The guy's shoes make a squooshy sound like his socks are wet.

"That *everything?*" the man asks. *That's what clerks always say,* Walk reminds himself, but he knows the words are meant differently for him. He's not sure why this bugs him so much. It happens all the time.

Back in the car, Walk slams the door and rips open the pastry with his teeth.

"*You* in a mood now?" Sylvia asks.

Walk doesn't answer.

When they get home, Sylvia gets out of the car and marches all around it to make sure nobody scratched up her baby. She does this every day.

"Jamal called," Sylvia says as she unlocks the door to their apartment.

Jamal's the cousin everyone figured would go to Harvard and end up some big important guy. Aunt Shandra always used to say: "You watch Jamal, Walk, you do what he does." Shan doesn't have kids but she has a million opinions on how they're supposed to be raised. She used to like Jamal, but now she's all over him about everything. Though he *is* acting kind of strange lately. He's either all secretive or trying to sell

21

you something. Jamal will sell you your own shoes right off your feet and while he's at it, your socks.

Walk grabs the phone and dials. "Hey, Jamal," Walk says.

"How you doin'? Look man, I'ma come over tonight, got something I want to talk to you about. Somethin' important."

Sylvia's in the bathroom with the shower on. "Can Jamal come over?" Walk shouts through the door.

"When?"

"Now."

"No." She turns the shower off. "I'm goin' out tonight. I don't want him over if I'm not here."

Walk goes back to the phone. "Can't," he tells Jamal.

"Why not?"

"Sylvia."

"This ain't your ordinary thing here. This a chance of a lifetime. You could be rich the end of this month you listen to me."

"You still owe me from the last time," Walk says.

"Oh *that*? That was nothin'. Don't pay any attention to that. *This*, this is good. This is so good."

"I can't," Walk says.

"Fine, man, fine. But you pass on this one, you be sorry. Everybody at school is doin' it . . . and they're all askin' about you, too."

"What you tell 'em?"

"I told 'em you're too good for us now."

"I always been too good," Walk says.

"Yeah, you butthead. Why'd I call, anyway?"

"I don't know, man."

"So hey, what's it like?" Jamal asks.

"Different. Really different. Kids go to Turkey for the summer and, you know, Barcelona and New Zealand."

"B.T. went to Ohio."

"He like it?"

"Said it was so hot it melted his shoes right off his feet. Call me when I can come over, okay?"

"Okay."

"Where you goin', anyway?" Walk asks Sylvia after he hangs up. She has the ironing board out and she's pressing her best red dress.

"Dinner."

"Who with?"

"With whom."

"You know what I mean."

"Yes, and I want you to say it correctly," she says.

"With whom."

"No one I'm interested in."

"Why you going, then?"

"Because," she says, her hand jumping around like it wants to hold a cigarette. She pops a piece of gum in her mouth. Sylvia quit smoking a year and a half ago. She puts a smiley face on the calendar every day she doesn't smoke.

Walk

Walk checks to make sure she has enough nicotine gum. "You're not going to smoke, are you?"

She chews hard. "Nope."

"Be home early?"

She laughs. "I ever home late? I left you a plate of chicken and mashed potatoes. All you have to do is warm it up. I don't want you going out and I don't want you inviting anyone in. Understand?"

Walk rolls his eyes. "Who am I going to invite in? I already told Jamal no."

"You know who I'm talking about."

"I play ball with guys from up the hill *once* and you're still makin' a federal case about it."

"I'm not doing anything of the kind. I'm simply stating the rules. Keep the door locked; stay inside. Any problems, call my cell."

"Okay, sure, I'll keep you posted: 6:05, chewing. 6:06, swallowing. 6:07, burping. 7:00, taking a leak."

She makes a yap, yap, yappin' motion with her hands, then she swings out the door, her skirt rustling all noisy when she walks. Her high heels clickety-clacking as they pop on and off her heels.

Sylvia goes out like dating is a holiday comes once a year. After every date she says: "Not a keeper. Wouldn't hold a candle to your dad." And that's the end of that until the next year.

Walk never met his dad. He was an Air Force casualty, died before Walk was born. It was "friendly fire" got him. Who thought that name up, anyway? Is it supposed to make him feel better that a friend shot his father?

What Walk has from his dad are three pictures. "How come that's all?" Walk asked Sylvia once. "Your husband, the daddy of your child, and all you have is three pictures? What, they didn't invent the camera yet?"

"Mr. Funnyman," Sylvia said.

Not one of them is a wedding picture, either. She married him, though. Sylvia's maiden name is Roodelman; she was ready to marry at eight months old just to get rid of that name.

Walk's dad was smart and he was slick, too. He could tell a girl she's butt ugly and make it sound like the best news she ever heard. His life was charmed, Sylvia said, and then he died.

One picture is of Climpton in his Cub Scout uniform. He's nine or so and he looks like he just tied your shirttail to the toilet flusher and he's waiting for you to find out. Number two has him with his arm around Sylvia. When Sylvia sees this one, she smiles and says, "He was a handsome devil, wasn't he?" Number three Walk calls *Climpton Jones and the Fence*; his dad was just leaning in that one. Leaning and thinking.

Walk would give every last CD he owns to know what was inside his dad's head right then.

SEVEN

Kirsten

My sweater shelf is neat now, too. I'm starting on my dresses when my cell rings. I can't flip it open fast enough. It's got to be Rory.

But it's not Rory, it's Gwyneth Paltrow asking me to support cystic fibrosis. Gwyneth Paltrow has never called me before. It sounds like she's really talking to me, too. I can't wait to tell Rory about this, but when I dial, her line goes right to voice mail. Not again. She's going to be sorry if Gwyneth Paltrow can't get through.

Now Kippy knocks her Kippy code. She says it's Morse code for "Kippy is here." Knowing Kippy it probably *is* Morse code for "Kippy is here."

I open the door and she comes in with a bag of books and her old tattered baby blanket. She settles in on my bed.

"Do all parents fight this much?" she asks.

"I don't think so."

Kip sighs an old-lady sigh—deep and long. "So why are they like this?"

I shake my head. "I dunno. It's a lot worse than it used to be."

She nods extra big like she's agreeing as much as she can.

Once I tried to tell my mom how much it bothers Kip when they fight. But she said, "Don't be silly, all parents fight. It's natural and all kids have to get used to it."

"Hey," I tell Kip, "you want to color my hand?"

I get out my washable markers and she begins to draw warts, chicken pox, and Band-Aids all up and down my arm.

"I wonder what leprosy looks like?" she asks as she begins work on my other arm.

She's just about done when there's another knock on the door. This will be my mother. She's due in to give me a little talking-to about eating Dad's ice cream.

"Come in," Kippy says before I can stop her.

But it's not her, it's him. He's brought his guitar along.

"Yay!" Kippy cheers, leaping off my bed to hug our father. I feel the same way. It's been such a long time since he's sung to us.

He slides the embroidered band around his shoulder. It says WAR IS NOT GOOD FOR CHILDREN AND OTHER LIVING THINGS. He sits down on my chair, takes out his pick, and slowly tunes each string. Kippy and I snuggle close together on my bed like we always do when he plays. Then he starts in with "Blowin' in the Wind,"

Kirsten

"Come Together," and "Eleanor Rigby." He doesn't know many songs and they are all ancient. But we don't care. The only part we don't like is when he stops.

"I love when he's our dad," Kippy whispers after he's gone.

"Yeah," I say. "Me, too."

EIGHT

Walk

The bell rings and Ms. Scrushy comes in. Ms. Scrushy is like a ball flying fast down the stairs. She walks fast, talks fast, even takes quick gulps from her water bottle. This is one wired woman—even her hair is wound tight.

Right away she reassigns the seats in alphabetical order. Yesterday they sat by zodiac signs. How's she going to seat them tomorrow? By blood type?

Walk takes his new seat. Brianna Hanna-Hines is right in front of him. She's wearing a SAVE THE SALMON T-shirt. She looks good, her hair all shiny . . . smells good, too—like coconuts. She should be in a commercial for something. Walk would buy it, whatever it is.

Ms. Scrushy hands out booklets. "Writers' notebooks," she says. "We will be writing in them the first ten minutes of class every day."

Jamal always tells Walk, in English class you got to write something sad: somebody died, you miss your grandpa, your momma works three jobs, boo-hoo, boo-hoo. Teachers eat that up with a big spoon. Walk wonders if Ms. Scrushy is the big-spoon type.

"Write the quote in your notebooks." She writes on the board. "Then write the first thing that comes to your head. This is warm-up writing. I want two paragraphs, minimum."

Walker Jones
September 1

"If you give a person a fish, he eats for a day. If you teach him to fish, he eats for a lifetime."

I don't know how to fish. I guess I'm going to starve.

I did own a goldfish once. He lived for a week and then I found him floating belly up. Nothing on Google about giving mouth-to-mouth to a goldfish. Fish are slimy; their mouths are too small. And what if he was dead? Who wants to put your lips on a dead fish's lips? Nobody likes their fish that much.

Sylvia said the Lord's Prayer. Then she flushed my fishy down the toilet. Sylvia taught me something important that day. How to flush. I will know this all my life now.

Walk wonders if Ms. Scrushy has a sense of humor. He thinks she does. People with large red glasses can't take themselves too seriously.

Ms. Scrushy has her glasses in her hand now. She's

waving them around as she talks to the librarian. The librarian's name is Mrs. Dora Perkins but Matteo said everyone calls her Dorarian the librarian. Walk tries to follow what she is saying, but he can't because now Brianna has her elbow on his desk.

Nice elbow.

Walk forces himself to concentrate on Dorarian. She's wearing lots of fake blue fur. Blue fur shoes. A blue fur vest.

Think blue fur. Do not think hot girl with elbow on his desk.

"I nominate Walk," Hair Boy says.

Uh-oh. For what?

"Anyone second the nomination?" Dorarian asks.

"I do," Jade says, shaking her two-toned hair.

"Good. Other nominations?" Dorarian looks around. "No other nominations. Walk, do you accept your position?" Dorarian's strange gold eyes bug out at him from behind her blue glasses.

Brianna is turned around staring at him, too. What has he been nominated for? Taking out the trash?

Walk spins off his best smile. "Yes, of course," he says.

"Good. First student council meeting tomorrow after school."

Walk taps Hair Boy's shoulder. "I'm the student council representative?"

Hair Boy laughs. "Yeah, dude, where you been?"

31

Walk

NINE

Kirsten

When my mom drops me off on Saturday, I see Rory's brown straight ponytail. She was late on Tuesday, but she didn't say she'd be here today. "Hey, Rory!" I try to catch up, walking as fast as I can without jiggling.

"Hey, Kirsten." She smiles.

"How come you didn't email?"

"Oh. Yeah. I had to do something," she mumbles.

"When's the talent show audition?"

"Next week."

"What are you going to sing?"

"'Do You Believe in Magic,'" she says.

"Really? I thought you hated that kind of little-kid stuff."

"I kinda do and I kinda don't," she says as if this explains everything. Her eyes search the drop-off.

"Don't they, like, play that on Radio Disney?" I ask.

"Rory! You little stinker." Brianna bursts into the

drop-off from the school door. "I've been looking all over for you."

"*You little stinker?*" I whisper to Rory. Rory and I save lines like this so we can crack up about them when we're alone.

"Brianna!" Rory's whole face glows. She hurries away from me.

My mouth hangs open.

"I'm so glad you're here," Rory tells Brianna, heading inside without even a glance in my direction.

Rory and Brianna? They aren't friends. That couldn't be right.

Rory must have felt uncomfortable because she knows I don't like Brianna. Poor Rory. She's trying to make the best of a bad situation. I should be super-friendly like it's no big deal? I head down the hall to Balderis's. Everyone else has started working except for Rory and Brianna, who are sitting in the back. "Hey." I giggle. "What are you guys doing?" I try to sound cool, like I don't really care.

Rory doesn't turn her head toward me.

"You must be joking," Brianna tells Rory. "That is like way over the top."

"Hello?" I say.

Rory's head is set permanently in Brianna's direction. She ignores me and keeps talking.

I look down at the jean skirt I'm wearing. I thought it looked good at home, but now I see it makes me

Kirsten

look like a semi—a mobile home made entirely of denim. All I need is a sign that says WIDE LOAD.

I take a wobbly breath and walk away.

The bathroom. Thank god for the bathroom.

I go in a stall and sit down. Rory must not have heard me.

But Rory did hear me. Rory is friends with Brianna Hanna-Hines. When did that happen?

I bite my tongue so I won't cry. It would be better to walk down the hall in nothing but a training bra and Little Mermaid underpants than bawl at school.

But I can't stay in here. Eventually someone will come looking for me. How embarrassing would that be?

I walk to the sink, splash water on my face, take a deep breath, and I go out.

TEN

Walk

Walk and Sylvia are on the freeway going to school. No traffic—it's Saturday—but Sylvia is going eleven miles an hour.

Sylvia punches the CD button, taps the steering wheel, fiddles with her earrings, load, eject, load, eject, won't even leave *Aretha* on for one whole song. She's always like this on the way to a funeral.

Sylvia is an ICU nurse at Children's Hospital. When one of the kids she takes care of dies, Sylvia goes to the funeral. If she were a sniffler, it wouldn't be so bad, but she has double-amp lungs. She shakes, she sobs, she moans, and Walk bolts for the parking lot, goes to visit the body, holds the body's hand—anything but sit with her when she's like that. Okay, so she loves her patients, but man, couldn't she switch to something where they don't all die?

Walk usually goes with her to keep her company, except today he has to help Balderis. "You okay without me?"

"Course. Do a good job, now."

"I'm helping him move; it's not a test."

She bites her bottom lip, carves lipstick off with her teeth. "Brothers can't—"

"Make it in this world unless we work twice as hard as everyone else," Walk finishes for her.

She taps the steering wheel with her nails.

Walk makes his hand into a mic and his voice high and scratchy like hers. "Keep your nose clean, mind your own business."

She rolls her eyes.

"I'm gonna be lifting books and carrying them. What do you want? 'Lifting, A. Carrying, A. Walking While Carrying, A plus.'"

She laughs. "Love you, now scat," she says as the car pulls up in front of school.

Walk hits the pavement, cuts through the main building, sees Matteo up ahead. "Matteo? What you doin' here, man? You weren't late."

"In case I am, though," Matteo says.

"Balderis givin' get-out-of-jail-free cards?"

A smile snakes across Matteo's lips. "Gotta be careful. You never know," he mutters.

They're almost to room 222 when the custodian sticks his head out of the library and looks Walk up and down.

"They should take me to jail; save us all a lot of time," Walk whispers. "Do they have a prison track at Mountain School?"

"Shut up!" Matteo whispers.

Walk snorts. "Whatever you say, Matteo Riadosa. What's your middle name, anyway?"

"Like I'm going to tell you."

"You got one worse than Wilburt? The 'Will' isn't so bad, but 'Burt'? No one named Burt but that puppet on *Sesame Street*. He's the paranoid one, too."

"A paranoid *Muppet*?" Matteo laughs.

Balderis is in the hall with a bandanna tied around his head. He's wearing an army jacket, too. Someone should tell him he's old. Let him down gently.

"Hi, Mr. Balderis," Walk says, checking out who else is here today. Kirsten, looking kinda lost, like she forgot her security blanket. Rory, the girl Kirsten is always talking to. And Brianna, the girl Matteo's all weird about.

It's not like Walk's supposed to get up close with white girls, anyway. Race doesn't matter, according to Sylvia Roodelman Jones, except for every hour of every day. She should give him a little cheat sheet. Are Chinese girls okay? How about Latin American? Half Jewish? A quarter Japanese? What about two shakes of Hindu? You need a calculator to figure it out.

It's not just girlfriends, either. All his bros got to be squeaky clean, get all As, and sing in a boys' choir—real high-pitched, too. She's terrified Walk'll turn into Neek, her best friend's kid, who's in the system again. *Juvi. Juvi. Juvi.* Walk keeps telling her, "Don't have to

37

worry, Momma. Before I go bad I'll let you know, send a Hallmark card ready-made for the occasion . . . 'On the Eve Your Son Messes Up.'"

Sylvia does not laugh.

Walk tosses his backpack in a pile and looks around to see what he can do. Kirsten is carrying one end of a projector screen; Matteo grabs the other.

Walk gets a stack of books and takes them out in the hall. He and Matteo haul one big ol' load after another. Balderis is the only teacher who has a whole library in his class and a couple of couches to boot.

Brianna comes in singing like she's got a film crew trailing her. Her cell rings; she's out again. Balderis doesn't say anything to her. Cells aren't allowed in class, not that she'd care, but you'd think Balderis would've been all over her for that. Maybe he's on Saturday behavior. Or maybe he thinks she's hot, too.

It's almost lunch by the time Balderis busts her. "Brianna, either get serious about this or go home. You have two tardies. I'm not excusing two tardies unless you put in some effort here."

"I've been here since nine o'clock this morning. I have been working *so* hard. I had to go tinkle and that's all. Ask anyone." Brianna looks around the room. "Right, Matteo?"

Matteo's eyes hit the floor; he nods his head.

"Liar," Walk whispers.

Matteo's brown cheeks flame up red.

"Hey, not that I blame you. Brianna says she's Mother Teresa, I'll back her right up." Walk laughs.

Matteo looks away.

Kirsten appears suddenly with a whiteboard. "Think this is going to take the whole day?"

"Seems like we're done," Walk tells her, "unless Balderis finds us something else to do . . . collate pages, erase pencil marks, wash his underwear."

Kirsten gets all giggly.

Walk sets his end down. "What, you don't want to wash his underwear?"

"Walk! Kirsten! Matteo! Back in room 222 *right now*," Balderis shouts, his face all red.

"Uh-oh . . . ," Walk tells Matteo.

"Yeah, what's up with him?"

Walk shakes his head. "Who knows, man? Who knows?"

Room 222 is empty. They spent all morning ripping the guts out. Brianna and Rory are sitting on the carpet in the back messing with each other's hair.

"All right," Balderis barks, his teeth clenched. He closes the door. "No one is leaving here until we find out who did this."

"Did what?" Rory asks.

"My wallet is missing. I put it in the back of the file cabinet drawer like I always do, but apparently I forgot to lock it."

Balderis's eyes move slowly across Rory, Brianna,

Kirsten, Matteo. But when he comes to Walk they shoot across his face.

Walk's chest gets tight like a hand is pressing on it. Balderis suspects *him* now?

He does.

ELEVEN

Kirsten

Mr. Balderis." Brianna waves her hand back and forth. "Excuse me, Mr. Balderis." Wavey-poo, wavey-poo. "I know who did it. It was that girl, Kirsten. Rory and I saw her."

I choke on my own spit. "Wh-What?"

Rory opens her mouth to answer. She looks at me for a second. My best friend, Rory Dunkel. The girl who knows all the words to "I'd Like to Teach the World to Sing," the girl who I taught how to use tampons and hook her bra in the back so she didn't have to hook it in front and shimmy it around like old ladies do.

Rory nods her head ever so slightly. Her eyes are glued to Brianna's face.

"Rory!" I can't stop looking at her. "Mr. Balderis . . . she's . . . it's a *lie.*"

"You're calling Rory a *liar?*" Brianna asks.

"No, but I . . . I didn't take anyone's wallet."

"All right," Balderis roars, his hand in the air.

"Rory, stand by the files. Brianna, over there. Walker, center of the room. Matteo, side wall. Kirsten, front row. Bring your backpack, roller bag, camelback, whatever the heck you have. I want everything spread out on the rug in front of you. *Now!*"

In my backpack are two bags of potato chips, a Snickers, and a bag of Famous Amos chocolate chip cookies. I spent my allowance at 7-Eleven.

Brianna weighs maybe eighty pounds on a fat day. Rory isn't fat, either, and she totally believes I have a glandular disorder. I can't let them see I eat this way.

I walk up to Balderis. "Mr. Balderis, I can't . . . No, it's, uh, private," I whisper.

Balderis's face gets small and tight like a fist.

"I—I have pr-private stuff in there."

He grabs my backpack and starts digging through.

"Just don't show everyone," I plead.

He pulls a brown square from my backpack. The Snickers. I'm going to die now. I'm never coming back to this stupid school ever again.

It takes a while for me to understand. He doesn't have a candy bar in his hand. He has a wallet.

TWELVE

Walk

I—I didn't—I didn't take your wallet...,"
Kirsten stutters, her head flat out on the desk like
she's roadkill.

Walk catches Matteo's eye and nods toward Kirsten.

Matteo shrugs like nothing he can do. Not his
problem.

"You're all excused. Except you, Kirsten." Balderis
hammers her name.

No one moves—not even Matteo's out the door,
but he's pointed that way.

"What's going to happen to her?" Brianna whispers all kittenish, fingering her hair.

Rory pushes for the door. Brianna waits a beat, but
when Balderis doesn't answer she's gone, too. Matteo's
out the door now. Walk's going to follow, but his shoes
don't cooperate. They're stuck to the floor.

This is none of your concern, Walker W. Jones. Walk
gives his mouth a little talking-to so it will keep itself
shut.

Balderis looks at Walk.

"She didn't do it, Mr. Balderis," Walk blurts out.

"How do you know?"

"She was with us most of the time."

"You know who did?"

"Nope."

Balderis's eyes are trying hard to read him. Makes Walk feel itchy all over. Balderis doesn't say anything. Not a word. Walk gets his feet moving, buzzes on down the hall.

"What happened?" Matteo asks.

"I stuck my fool neck out."

Matteo's lips roll up into a big fat smirk.

"Not one word about it, O Perfect One," Walk tells him.

Matteo seals his lips, but his laugh bursts like a sneeze out his nose.

"What are you laughin' at?"

"You. Got your finger in everything."

"Me?"

"Yeah. You been here what? A week? And you're already on the student council, the debate team, and the girls are into you big time."

"Sure, yeah. Well, of course."

"I'm not kidding, man. But you act like you don't even notice, like you're everybody's friend. Even Kirsten's."

"She's not my friend."

"Why you stick your neck out for her, then?"

"I just don't think she did it, okay?"

Matteo nods. "Me either . . . You think she's cute?"

"Not my type . . . you?"

Matteo's face blazes red. "Nope."

"You do, don't you?"

"No, I don't."

Walk puts his hands up. "Whatever you say, man. Whatever you say."

At dinner, Sylvia and Walk eat at one end of the table. The other end is piled up with schoolwork. Sylvia teaches two nursing classes, so she always brings home big stacks of papers and marks them with her purple pen. "Purple kinder than red," she says. "Yeah, right," Walk tells her.

Walk takes a gulp of milk. "Some girl got accused of stealing Balderis's wallet today."

"Really?"

"I told Balderis I didn't think she did it."

Sylvia winds spaghetti around her fork. "You know who did?"

"Nope."

"But you think you do." She nods her head, answering for Walk.

"I just don't think it was her."

"You got a thing for her?"

"No."

One of her eyebrows raises up.

45

"No!"

She nods. Her face relaxes. "So this isn't any of your business, but you're in the middle of it any-hoo. That's my Walk." She slides the last piece of garlic bread onto his plate. "But hey, I sure rather have a big-hearted son than one with a shriveled old thing in there." She thumps his back. "Girl got a name?"

"Kirsten."

"Kirsten. What's her last name?"

"McKenna."

Sylvia's mouth drops open. She clamps it shut.

"What?" Walk asks.

"I haven't heard about her before."

"Remember Monday? We were late because you were driving the 350 like it has training wheels, then Kirsten's mom's minivan—that silver one—almost creamed the man in the drop-off, *remember*?"

"Vaguely."

"Kirsten was late, too. That's why we ended up helping Balderis today."

Sylvia nods her head, but she's biting her lip the way she does when Aunt Shandra wants to borrow money.

"You know something about her?" Walk asks.

Sylvia grabs the remote, flicks on the TV, and stares at it. "Nope," she says.

"Nothin'?"

She keeps staring at the screen.

"What?"

She sighs. "I met Kirsten's mom at that new-parent party. Didn't much care for her."

"Why?"

"Just didn't," she says, punching the volume up too loud.

Walk

THIRTEEN

Kirsten

Every time I look up at Balderis he looks so angry, I put my head back in my hands. I just want to get out of here. I don't care how. I'm going to start my life over again. Do they have witness protection when you're in the seventh grade?

"Do you want to tell me what happened?" he asks.

"I don't know how your wallet got in there, Mr. Balderis."

"Why didn't you want to open your backpack?"

"Because I had all that food," I whisper.

My hand shakes as I unzip the second pocket of my backpack. I can't bear to take it all out, so I give him a quick look, then zip it up fast. I feel like I've let him inspect my underwear drawer.

My face burns. "The cookies, the chips . . . they're for my sister," I mutter.

"Oh." He nods, stroking a sideburn. "Do you think someone planted the wallet in your backpack?"

"Brianna, not Rory. Rory is my friend." My voice cracks when I say this. I can hardly get the sentence out.

"Oh." He sighs.

"Are you going to call the police?" I whisper.

"No, I'm not going to call the police. Frankly I have no idea what to make of this, Kirsten. I'm going to write it up. Then I'll turn it over to Mr. Fishhouse."

Mr. Fishhouse . . . the principal. This is good news. All he can do is expel me. He can't lock me up for the rest of my life.

"Let him deal with it on Monday."

Monday . . . no problem. I won't be at school on Monday. I won't be at school ever again. "Can I go?" I ask.

He nods. "I'd like to believe you, Kirsten. I really would."

I stand up. "Yes, sir," I say. I've never called anyone sir in my whole life.

When I leave the door crashes closed behind me. It's one of those heavy spring-loaded doors that sound like the end of the world when they shut.

Kirsten

FOURTEEN

Walk

At church the next day Walk sees his cousin, Jamal, slumped down in a pew. "Hey, what you doin' here, Jamal?"

"Man got to go to church."

"Oh yeah. Since when?"

Jamal shrugs.

Walk looks down at Jamal's new Nikes. "Where you get those? How much they cost you?"

"Two hundred. But I sell 'em to you for one forty-nine."

"We're not the same size."

"One forty-nine. You can wear two pairs of socks, man," Jamal says.

"Gotta wear five pair. You got bigger feet than God."

"God have big feet?" Jamal asks.

"Yeah, bro, don't you know anything?" Walk tells him. "The guy means well, but his feet are too big and they step all over people, squash them flat."

"You talk to the rev about this?"

Walk shakes his head. "My own personal theory, man."

Jamal laughs. "If you're interested, I got some business."

"Last time you say that, you sell the rug out from under us."

"That was once, man. And it was only because I got a good price for it." Jamal's smile shows all in his eyes. His mouth is straight as a toothpick.

"We livin' on the floor now. Hard as rock," Walk tells him.

"Look, I wanna show you something I've been workin' on."

"For real?"

Jamal nods. "How 'bout Tuesday I come over show you?"

"Can't Tuesday. Student council meeting."

Jamal snorts. "On student council *already?*"

Walk shrugs.

Jamal nods and nods, watching Walk. "You like that new school?"

Walk shakes his head. "I'd be back at City in a hot minute if it weren't for Sylvia. You know—"

"Yeah, you would," Jamal interrupts, his lids low over his eyes.

"I would! You don't—"

"Sure," he snorts, cutting Walk off.

The choir's up front. One voice humming in the

Walk

microphone. Then—*boom*—both electric pianos and the chorus of voices lift the whole place up.

During the service, Jamal's head flops back. He's snoring and drooling on a brand-new, blue upholstered pew. Walk sees Aunt Tanesha glaring at Jamal. She's in the choir or she'd be on him in a flash.

A few minutes later, Aunt Shandra storms over clickety-click, clickety-click in her hot pink pointy-toed shoes. She slaps him on the side of the head, her bracelets jingle-jangling, then slaps him again. He wakes up for a minute, but by the time the rev is done, he's asleep again.

On the way home, Sylvia starts in. "So what did Jamal say?"

"Nothin'."

"I saw you talking to him."

"We talked about shoes."

"You need to tell me what you know. Shan's worried. Tanesha's worried. He's into something he shouldn't be." She shakes her head. "Kid's got his whole life in front of him if he doesn't screw it up."

"He's just doin' business like always. You know Jamal."

"Always trouble when a kid's got secrets like that. If he was proud of what he was doing, we'd be hearing about it."

Walk shrugs.

"You don't know anything?" Sylvia asks.

"Nope," he says. "Nothing."

FIFTEEN

Kirsten

My eyes are puffy. My nose is red. I look as if I've been thrown in the washer and slapped around in there. I've been crying practically since I got home from Balderis's yesterday.

My mother has asked me three times if everything is all right. "Just cramps," I tell her. That's the nice thing about your period. All you do is say the word and people back away. I know Kippy knows the truth, though. She has stacked four boxes of Kleenex outside my door.

I go online, again.

How could u do this 2 me?

Send.

What have I ever done 2 u?

Send.

I'm never going 2 talk 2 u again.

Send.

*I will never ever 4give u. I might pretend I
do, but I won't.*

Send.

I've called Rory's house maybe fifty times. "You've
reached the Dunkel household. If you'd like to leave a
message for Rebecca, press one; Arthur, press two;
Rory, press three." I hang up. Rory wouldn't call me
back, anyway. My only hope is to get her mom.

Now the phone rings, but it's my father. "Kirsten?
Everything okay?"

"Yeah, fine," I say. "Where are you?"

"I'm still at the fund-raiser. Will you tell your mom?"

"Uh-huh."

"How's school going? Starting out on the right foot
this year?"

"Sure, Dad, sure."

When he hangs up, I call the Dunkels again. Still
nothing. It's 5:30 Sunday night by the time the real Rebecca Dunkel answers. My voice pounces on her. "I
need to talk to Rory."

"Kirsten. How are you?"

"Fine. Is Rory there?"

"She isn't. But I will certainly let her know you
called."

I don't like the way she says this. Rory will never call me.

I wonder if I could walk to her house. But then what would I do when I get there? Sit on her? Let her hamster out?

Before I can figure it out, my mom comes in.

"Honey." She sits on my bed. "Are things going okay at school?"

Oh great, now she knows something. "Why?" I ask.

"Just wondering."

God, I hate when she lies.

She sighs. "I just happened to be talking to Rebecca and she said—"

"You just *happened* to be talking to her?"

My mother's head moves back. Her eyes move fast from side to side. "That's right."

I roll my eyes. "She said what?"

"There had been some problem at school. She wasn't sure about the details. Rory seemed pretty upset. Was there a problem?"

I can't tell my mom about the wallet *and the food*. I would rather die.

I take a breath. "Rory is acting weird."

She looks over her glasses. "You guys had a little tiff? Is that it?"

I shrug.

She seems to take this as a yes. Her lips pucker like

Kirsten

she's thinking it all out. "Rebecca said she'd try to find out more. She said she'd call me back."

"Mom!" I plead. She means well, but I really wish she'd leave me alone. I don't need her help on this. I'm almost thirteen.

"This is important. They're my friends, too, Kirsten," she says.

When it's time for bed, she's back with her bowl of air-popped popcorn. She grabs my *Seventeen*, places it on my duvet, and sets the bowl on top of it. "Here's what's happening. Rory is starting to spend time with Madison, Brianna, Maya, and Lauren. She says you don't like these girls. Is that true?"

I shrug.

"Well, they seem to think you don't. Rebecca says they don't trust you."

They don't trust *me*?

"Girls like to know that you're one of them. And when you strike out on your own the way you do . . ." She sighs. "People get suspicious. And I guess none of them liked that Nellie girl you were friends with last year. The one who moved away."

The tears well up in my eyes. "Sure, Mom. This is all my fault."

"I'm not saying this is your fault. It's just one of those things."

"Just one of those things" means: This sucks and you have to put up with it.

"But when people don't trust you, they stay away. Rebecca says these are nice girls. Brianna's mom, Jacqueline, is cochair of the auction. She's quite charming. And Maya's mom is a chatterbox—so bubbly and fun. Lauren's mom I don't know very well. But Madison's mom is a real go-getter.

"Rebecca says Rory's ready to branch out. Have a larger circle of friends, which I think is very healthy." She looks around my room. "Everyone wants to be popular, Kirsten. You can't blame Rory for that."

"I can't blame Rory? Whose mother are you?"

"You know I'm on your side, Kirsten, but if you want just Rory as your friend, I think you're going to be disappointed. You have to be a part of the whole group." Her shoulders settle into this.

I sink my teeth into the inside of my cheek. "Everyone knows Brianna isn't nice."

"Well, Rebecca says that you haven't been all that nice to *her*. She says Brianna is a natural-born leader, but she's very sensitive."

"Brianna *sensitive*?"

"She's very involved with the Save the Salmon movement. She cares deeply about . . ."

"Fish?"

"The environment," my mom says. "Look, the thing is, you just want to be one of the crowd for a while. One of the crowd, but you have to have a little something they want, too." She smiles. "You know, I saw the cutest boots at Nordstrom. You have a day off

Kirsten

from school tomorrow. Why don't we hop in the car and take a ride to the mall and try them on?"

I know my mom's trying. I know she is. But I've seen the pictures of her when she was twelve. She was thin. She was beautiful. She was an ice-skating champion and she had a million friends. The only thing I'm good at is Nintendo 64, which no one even plays anymore. Plus I have every episode of *Friends* practically memorized and my closet is also very neat.

How do I tell her that I'm a loose piece that doesn't fit anywhere? How do I say the world is whole without me?

"Sure, Mom," I tell her.

When she goes out, she's smiling like she's just earned 150 mother points for solving this for me.

The door closes behind her. The room is dark. I stare at the line of light leaking through the bottom of the door.

SIXTEEN

Walk

Sylvia is at the Y doing her Jazzercise class. Walk has the door wide open, the fan on high, but it doesn't help. It's really hot today. Why didn't he go with Sylvia? He could be in the pool right now instead of sweating over his homework.

Jamal pulls up in a black SUV with tinted windows. He's up front and this big Terminator guy's driving. Jamal has friends who drive? He's only thirteen.

B.T., who was in City with Walk, jumps out of the back. B.T. always acts cool like he doesn't know Walk. Today he's pulling along a little suitcase on wheels. What's he got that for? Is he moving in here?

Walk slides his homework under the chair cushion.

"What you doin' here, Jamal?" Walk asks.

"That's all you got for me? Where is the love, man?"

Jamal's boys plunk down in the living room. The Terminator guy grabs the remote.

"No AC?" B.T. scowls.

Walk shrugs.

The Terminator flips through the channels. Stops at *Rugrats*. "Hey, man, I love these little dudes." He pulls off his do-rag and settles in.

"Got some product to show you," Jamal tells Walk. "Really fine stuff. Not goin' to see this every day." He nods to B.T. B.T. unzips the suitcase.

"Product? What are you talkin' about, Jamal?" Walk asks.

"Tryin' to make some money, man. This is how you do it. I'ma show you." He cocks his small head. Earrings glisten in each ear.

Sweat drips down Walk's chest. He looks at the clock. "Sylvia be home any minute."

"So?" Jamal says.

"I don't do this stuff, Jamal."

"Everybody does this stuff. Don't you know anything?"

"Jamal, c'mon. Not here."

"This is how white people get rich. Seriously." Jamal smiles at him.

"No, it isn't."

"They don't get their hands dirty. They get other people do it for them. I'ma let you buy it first. Then we'll talk opportunities. This is a path paved with gold, man. *Paved with gold.*"

B.T. is unloading boxes now, different size boxes. All with one word on the top: AMWAY.

Laundry detergent, dishwashing detergent, brass cleaner, toilet cleaner, floor cleaner, sink cleanser.

Jamal nods. "Soap, man. First you sell. Then you get other people workin' for you and you know what happens when they sell? You make money without doin' one thing. Just sit on your booty and the money pours in."

"This is soap?" Walk asks.

"Not just soap. Best stuff there is. You can't buy this in any store anywhere. Not on the Web, either. You can only buy it from me."

"Yeah?" Walk says.

"Isn't anybody doesn't need soap. It's the American dream, man, right here. I've been to a weekend. They told me all about it."

Walk

SEVENTEEN

Kirsten

K irsten! Get up!" my mom calls from downstairs. I stick my head under the covers.

"I've got the flu. I'm going to throw up," I tell her when she knocks on my door.

"Honey, Rory just wants more friends. That doesn't mean she doesn't want to be *your* friend. You two have had spats before and you've always patched them up."

My mother sounds so reasonable. I want to believe she's right.

I take a deep breath and reach for my brand-new boots. I didn't buy the Nordstrom ones because I couldn't get them over my calves. They just scrunched down like sloppy socks. But I got these other ones at Macy's. They're ankle high, real leather, and incredibly cute. If you took a picture of my feet, you wouldn't even know I'm fat.

"Kirsten!" I pull the duvet back over my head.

"Honey?" My mom pokes her head in my door. "We're going to be late."

"I'm sick, Mom. I have the wastebasket right here. I'm going to throw up any minute. Any second!"

"Are you sure this isn't about Rory?" she asks, her eyes full of pain.

"I'm sure." I nod with too much enthusiasm.

My mom sighs and walks out. A few minutes later she's back, with the phone in her hand. "Kirsten, it's Rory. She wants to talk to you."

The phone hasn't rung. My mother called her mother. Can this get any more humiliating? I sit up in bed, take the phone, and wait until my mom leaves the room.

"Rory." My voice cracks.

"Brianna made me. She *forced* me," Rory says. "You have to forgive me, Kir. You have to."

Rory had a good reason. She did.

"You'll never believe what happened. Never," she says.

"Why did Brianna do it?" I ask.

"I'll tell you all about it *at school*. Your mom's going to drive us. C'mon, Kir, don't worry. This is all going to be fine."

It's so foggy on the way to Rory's house, my mom has her headlights on. She has to go really slow or she'll slam into someone on Rory's twisty road. Yesterday,

Kirsten

it was blistering hot; today the fog came in and it's freezing.

I read to Kippy from *All About Electrical Storms.* She knows how to read as well as I do, but she still likes me to read to her. "Read the part about getting electrocuted in the bathtub, please!" she begs.

I've been reading out loud for the last five minutes but not a single word has entered my brain. My mom pulls into the carport next to Rory's mom's Mercedes SUV then backs out to turn around. I stay where I am next to Kippy and make Rory climb over me. I know this is rude but I don't care. I don't care that Rory sees me holding Kippy's hand, either. So what if she thinks I'm a baby. So what.

Rory gives a little wave to my mom. "Hi, Rachel." There's something so girlfriendy about the way Rory says my mom's name. This has always bothered me a little. Now it bothers me a lot.

Rory's eyes track to the long handwoven sweater I'm wearing that's really my mom's. She's never let me borrow it before and I'm really hoping it stays foggy, so I can keep it on all day. "Kirsten, you look so nice."

"She got new boots," Kippy blurts out. "See!" She points to my feet.

"Yeah. They're cool." Rory looks sideways at me—a scared sneak of a look.

"Aren't they darling?" my mom asks into the rear-view mirror.

"Rachel, my mom says to tell you she checked with Brianna's mom and Thursday morning right after drop-off is fine for the auction meeting."

"Perfect," my mom chirps.

This all sounded better on the phone. Like maybe Rory really did feel sorry. Like maybe it *was* all Brianna's fault.

When my mom pulls into the drop-off, I climb out and Kippy squeezes hard before she lets go.

"Thanks for the ride, Rachel. Bye, Kippy," Rory says.

The door closes. Kippy waves.

Don't leave me here. Please, couldn't you homeschool me? But my mom has already pulled away.

"So." I can't look Rory straight in the eye.

"It was a mistake, Kirsten. An honest mistake."

I snort. "A mistake?"

"I thought I saw you take the wallet. But I was mistaken."

"What, it was my evil twin you saw?"

"Very funny."

"You said Brianna made you do it."

"She did." Rory's eyes are round. "She said she had to know if I was going to be their friend or not. She said it was all in fun and if you were really my friend you'd understand."

"*In fun?*"

Rory gets out her inhaler and puts it in her mouth. "Look"—she takes a gaspy breath—"I don't want to

65

be in the middle of this. I just want to be everybody's friend. That's what nobody understands."

"You weren't responsible. You were just along for the ride."

"I didn't do anything."

Rage flashes inside me. "Brianna put Balderis's wallet in my backpack, right? And then you lied and said I stole it. That wasn't anything?"

"I said I *thought* I saw you do it."

"That doesn't make sense, Rory."

"You don't know what I thought, Kirsten."

I scuff my boots on the pavement. "So what are you going to tell the principal?"

"That I thought I saw you take the wallet, but I was mistaken."

"And Brianna, what is she going to say?"

Rory's cheek twitches. "How should I know what she's going to say? Look, it's not like *I'm* in this group. Madison is the only one who really likes me. I have to be careful, you know."

"Careful, huh? And what about me?"

"I've been telling them how nice you are."

"I thought you hated Brianna."

"I never said that."

"Only a million times."

Rory shrugs. "Look," she whispers like we're sharing a big secret, "they might give you a try. Your mom is pretty hooked in. She's already called my mom and Madison's mom and Brianna's mom."

"They might give me a try? *Because of my mom?*"

"If you want to be friends with us, maybe you can be. Just don't tell your mom again, all right? My mom, like, wigs over stuff like that."

"Rory! Kirsten!" Brianna is hurrying toward me, her cell in her hand. "I am so sorry. But I've already talked to Fishhouse about it. We've got it all squared away. And man, do you look cute. Look at those boots. Can I do your hair at lunch, because I'm thinking you'd look just darling with a wrap! Isn't she cute, Rory?" Brianna pets my hair like I'm a dog. "She is so cute."

"Thanks," I say. "But, um, what did you get squared away? I mean, what did you say to the principal?"

Brianna shrugs. "I just explained how we were playing hot potato with Balderis's wallet, which we should not have been doing. Definitely should not have." She shakes her head. "It just happened to end up in your backpack. It was naughty of us, wasn't it, Rory?"

Rory nods.

"But since no money was taken and since I was '*proactive*' about '*taking responsibility*' for my behavior . . . That's what Fishhouse said. He said he'd take into consideration that he heard from me first, rather than from Balderis. And I apologized for getting carried away. You know how kids are."

Rory giggles.

Brianna clicks her lips, "Tsk, tsk, tsk. Then he said he was a kid once, too." She smiles. "Once they say that, you know you got 'em. And when they say, 'But if it happens again, there will be real trouble,' you know you got it, like, totally wrapped up. So that's it." She brushes her hands together like she's wiping herself free of this. "We're done. You don't even have to talk to him."

"Really?" I'm impressed despite myself.

Brianna smiles. "Yeah. Don't worry, Kirsten." She pats my arm. "I took care of it. It's over." She smiles like she knows what a cutie-pie she is.

"Balderis isn't going to say anything? Fishhouse isn't going to call me in?"

Brianna shakes her head. "Fishhouse isn't going to call you in. Balderis? He's a little turd—a turdette. Turdité." She looks at Rory.

Rory laughs.

"But he got his wallet back," Brianna says, "so what does he care?"

"So all I do now is show off my footwear?" I point my toe.

"Exactly," Brianna says.

"I told you we had it worked out," Rory whispers to me.

I try not to smile at Rory. Try not to walk with her and Brianna. I'm not a part of their crowd. But my new boots trot to catch up.

EIGHTEEN

Walk

On Monday Walk gets his butt in his seat in plenty of time. He won't be late again, that's for sure.

Brianna is out in the hall. She comes in with Madison, Lauren, Rory, and Kirsten. Kirsten? She's one of *them* now? Must have been some catfight got that straightened all out. Walk looks for bite marks, scratches, places been chewed up. But no, they're smiling like they're best girlfriends.

Balderis is looking at Kirsten, too. His eyebrows jump off his face and his mouth hangs open. He doesn't get it, either. What's with these girls, anyway? They all nuts?

NINETEEN

Kirsten

My mom picks me up from school.

"Where's Kippy?" I ask.

"After-school care," my mom answers.

"Why?"

"You're going to the doctor."

"I am? What doctor?"

"A psychiatrist. She specializes in eating disorders."

"Oh great, now you think I'm a psycho?"

"No, I don't think you're a psycho."

"Other people's moms don't haul them off to headshrinkers. Other people's moms take them shopping. That is probably what Rory and her mom are doing right now."

"I just took you shopping."

"Oh, yeah, you're right. Thanks."

My mom glances over at me, her whole face open and hopeful. "How is Rory, anyway?"

I stare out the passenger side window. "Mom, maybe you and Dad should go to a therapist. Not me."

"Your dad doesn't believe in therapy. He thinks it's self-indulgent."

"He's right," I say. "Absolutely."

My mom rolls her eyes. We pull into an office park. I follow her inside and up a back stairwell that smells suffocatingly stale.

I hang back, going slower and slower until I come to a complete halt. My mom waits at the top of the stairs.

"Kirsten, you have no idea the strings I had to pull to get you this appointment. Dr. Markovitz isn't accepting new patients."

"Why didn't you tell me about it?"

"I didn't want you to get nervous."

"*Nervous?*"

"Okay, I wanted you to give it a chance."

"Mom, you and Dad are the ones acting weird. Not me. Why are you making this my problem?" The stairwell echoes my words.

"Don't you want to be thin?"

"Mommmmmm!"

"Okay, okay . . . just go this once?" She holds up one finger. "If you don't want to go again, I promise I won't make you, all right?"

We get to the waiting room and my mom pushes a little light by the name Dr. Marilyn Markovitz. I flip through *Seventeen*. ARE YOU A JERK MAGNET? BUTT-FRIENDLY BATHING SUITS. WHAT TO DO ABOUT THUNDER THIGHS.

Kirsten

When Dr. Markovitz appears I see she's normal weight. On the tall side, too. She can probably eat a dozen Krispy Kremes and not gain weight.

Dr. Markovitz nods to my mom. "Why don't you and I spend a few minutes together, then Kirsten and I will talk."

I go back to *Seventeen*. I'm halfway through the "How to Tell If He's a Jerk" quiz when Mom comes out. She nods to me; her lips waver on the edge of a smile.

"You're feeding me to the dogs," I whisper as I follow Dr. Markovitz's efficient gray pantsuit. The business kind. Not the grandma kind. Her office is surprisingly unoffice-like, though. It's all pink like the inside of your mouth.

"How's school been going?" Dr. Markovitz asks after introducing herself.

"Fine," I say when I've settled into a low pink-flowered chair.

"And home?"

"Fine."

"Do you know why you're here?"

"I'm unsightly? I'm the wart in the house."

She smiles. "That wasn't exactly how your mother put it, but yes, she did indicate you've gained weight recently."

I stare at a shelf in the back full of little-kid toys. There's a Slinky, a wagon full of brightly colored blocks, a Raggedy Ann, and a barn with plastic animals. Being a little kid was a lot more fun than being twelve.

"Do you feel comfortable with the weight gain?"

What kind of question is that? *Sure, I just love being fat. It's every girl's dream.*

"Your mom said you had an incident over your father's ice cream. She says it's happened before."

Heat chases up my neck. I focus my eyes on a pink wicker wastebasket and imagine myself home in my basement chair in front of my TV.

"It's interesting you ate *his* ice cream."

"My mom doesn't eat ice cream."

"She said you and your dad used to be quite close."

I shrug.

She waits.

"Everybody loves my dad."

"And what about you?"

"He's not home very much anymore. Besides, it's easier to be close to your dad when you're a little kid. It's like babies. Anything is possible with a baby. That's why everyone loves them. But once you're twelve it's all over."

"It's all over *at twelve?* Why do you say that?"

"You're already, you know, formed. You're not going to all of a sudden turn into Albert Einstein or anything."

"Does your father want you to be Albert Einstein?"

"No."

Kirsten

73

"But you don't think he's happy with who you are?"

I shrug. "He always calls us his brilliant daughters, but I know he only means Kippy."

"Kippy is really smart?"

"Really smart," I say.

Dr. Marilyn Markovitz nods and says nothing for the longest time. Much longer than you're supposed to wait in conversations. What is the matter with this lady, anyway?

"Your mother says you get along extremely well with Kippy. Is that what you think?"

I nod.

"She also said you're having trouble making friends with the girls at school."

"She's wrong. I have lots of friends," I snap.

"So why do you think you've gained thirty pounds in the last four months?"

"It's not that much."

She looks at me, her lids low over her eyes.

"I eat too much." I pick at a thread in my skirt. "So where's the diet?"

She shakes her head. "No diet."

"No diet? Does my mom know that?"

"You're a bright girl, Kirsten. You don't need another diet."

"No, I'm not. You should check out my grades."

"I don't need to. I can tell by what you say and the way you say it that you're smart. Your mom can, too."

I shrug and try to pretend I have no feelings about this, but my eyes are beginning to leak.

"Is it possible the eating is a way to divert attention from your parents' problems?"

I shake my head. "It's just that . . . it's just"—I look directly at her for the first time—"I want things the way they used to be."

"When your father really did think you were brilliant and your parents didn't fight?"

I nod a tiny nod like suddenly I am as small as Kippy.

My nose is running, but I'm not crying. I'm not. "I'm ready to go now." I stand up.

"So how was it?" my mom asks when we're walking back down the stale-air stairwell. "What happened? Tell me everything."

"Nothing happened," I mumble. "And I'm not going back."

Kirsten

TWENTY

Walk

At lunch Walk is sitting with Matteo, Hair Boy, and Jade. Jade is busy reading Hair Boy's palm. "You're next," she tells Matteo.

Matteo makes the sign of the cross like she's a vampire and should stay away.

"C'mon, Study Boy, loosen up," Jade tells him as a milk carton comes flying through the air dribbling drops of milk on Matteo's head on its way to the trash can.

"Hey!" Matteo barks.

Walk turns around and there is Madison with a big stupid smile on her face and Brianna holding her stomach, she's laughing so hard. Matteo bites his lip. His eyes smolder. He turns back to the door, waiting for Dorarian to walk through. She opens the library after she eats her lunch. They know it's open when she walks through the cafeteria to get hot water for her tea.

"Do another one like that," Brianna says.

Madison grabs another carton and throws this one

behind her back to a second trash can. She lands this one, too. The girl has game, gotta give her that.

"You're such a guy," Brianna tells her.

Matteo turns back around.

Madison makes two more baskets. She's out of empties, so she grabs the carton of a kid with green pool hair. It hits the trash rim and sprays milk everywhere.

"Hey!" another kid yells, his new Nikes sprayed with milk.

Then suddenly Dorarian is there, holding her blue fur-covered thermos. She looks at Madison, Brianna, and the milk-splattered floor. "Whoever did this needs to clean it up."

"It wasn't us, Dorarian," Brianna says. "It was—" She looks around. "Martin Luther King, here," she mutters just loud enough for Walk to hear.

"What?" Dorarian's hands are on her hips.

"You gonna say that again so everybody can hear?" Walk asks.

"Matteo," Brianna says.

"Matteo?" Dorarian frowns. She turns to them. "Did you do this?"

"Yes," Matteo tells the floor.

"No, you didn't," Walk snarls.

"Shut up," Matteo hisses.

Dorarian's eye is twitching. She knows they're hustling her, but she can't seem to figure out what to do about it. "Come with me, Matteo," she says finally.

Walk shakes his head. He can't believe this.

Walk

"Matteo," Walk whispers when Matteo comes back with a mop, "what's the matter with you?"

"I dropped my milk."

Walk groans. "Come on, man!"

"You just didn't see," Matteo says, pushing the mop so hard he's practically breaking the head off.

Later when Walk and Matteo head for the gym, they see Balderis standing at the end of the lockers talking to Dorarian.

"Hey, Walk, Matteo," Mr. Balderis calls, "you have a minute?"

"Sure," Walk says.

"Mrs. Perkins here said something happened at lunch today she thinks I should talk to you two about."

Dorarian glances quickly at them, then slips back into the library.

"You want to tell me what happened?" Balderis asks.

"Nothing happened," Matteo says.

"We ate lunch," Walk says.

Balderis looks from Matteo to Walk and back again. "That's it? Nothing happened in the cafeteria with you and Brianna and Madison?"

They shake their heads.

Balderis scratches at his sideburns. "All right. You need help, you let me know."

After he goes, Walk looks at Matteo, wishing he'd say something about this, but Matteo doesn't say a word.

When Matteo closes up like this it makes Walk miss Jamal. Jamal would tell him what was going on. The old Jamal would anyway. Is this what happens when you grow up—more and more people shut you out?

TWENTY-ONE

Kirsten

On Saturday Kippy goes to her best friend Sam's house. I am glad Kip has Sam. They are like your left and right shoe, a perfect fit in the box. Were Rory and I ever like this, I wonder as my mom and I drive from Sam's.

In the car my mom has been nattering on and on about trees. I've mostly tuned her out, when suddenly I see what she's been talking about. The big beautiful oak tree in our front yard is gone. The yard is a total mess, and yard guys are feeding branches to a mulcher.

My dad is standing on the stump where the tree used to be. He's a tall man, but he looks short compared to a tree.

"Sudden Oak Death!" my mom shouts over the noise. "The tree guy said I had to cut it down."

"Did he also say you should do it without talking to me?" my father yells back.

"Don't pretend you care what happens here," she shouts.

"Please tell me you didn't do this to get back at me."

"Don't think I'd stoop that—"

I run inside and slam the door. The grinding noise stops.

I head straight for our suitcases and pull out the one my dad always uses. When my father comes inside, I'm hauling it up the stairs. "You going somewhere?"

My face gets hot. "No."

"Why do you have my suitcase?"

"You're not going to be needing it, right?" I grip the handle hard so my hand won't shake.

"Not today."

I nod. "Kippy's going to be sad about the tree."

"It was sick."

"Was it?"

"Ask your mother, Kirsten."

"Ask your mother. Ask your father. Ask your—"

"All right. I get the point."

"You going to get divorced?"

He winces. "Your mom and I are going through a rough patch. We'll get through it."

"Rough patch, my foot."

He bites his lip and looks away.

"What's the suitcase for?" he asks.

"So you can't use it."

"You're too old to play games like that."

"I know."

He breaks out his most charming smile. "You

81

know how much I love my brilliant daughters." He puts his arm around me and tries to hug me, but the hug is like two boards knocking against each other.

Even so I don't want him to stop—only he does because his beeper goes off.

He looks at the number, then calls in. "Dr. Mac here, what can I do for you? Yes, yes, okay." He nods, grabs his BlackBerry, and enters some notes. "I'll be there as soon as I can."

He's gone now. The house is quiet. My mother sighs. "Can't live with him. Can't live without him," she says.

TWENTY-TWO

Walk

It's Open House at Mountain School. Walk, Matteo, and some girl got asked to come and talk about the project they did on the Supreme Court. Otherwise Open House is just for parents and prospective parents.

Matteo said he did Open House last year and it was boring; he just sat around. None of the parents said much. The prospective parents were the only ones who wanted to know stuff.

Sylvia is ironing up a storm. Even ironed Walk's socks. "Can't have you lookin' like something the cat dragged in," she mutters.

As soon as they get to school, she's all over him about his essay. "None of the other kids' essays are handwritten."

"It's up on the wall. Only the best ones are up there," Walk tells her like she's stupid.

She doesn't answer.

"Gotta get a new printer if you want me to type everything."

"It works."

"It doesn't," Walk snorts, but Sylvia is already moving on.

Parents come and go. None of them ask Walk and Matteo anything. They ask the girl all their questions.

"Your parents coming?" Walk asks Matteo.

Matteo shakes his head. "My mom has to work."

"What about your dad?"

"Not his, you know"—Matteo shrugs—"kind of thing."

A man starts reading Walk's essay. So far no one has read all the way through, but this guy puts one hippie-sandal foot on a chair and settles in like he's doing his own word count, spell-check, fact-check, and grammar-check, too.

Hippie Sandals nods his head. "Nice work," he says.

"Thanks," Walk says.

"Anything else yours?"

Walk points to the current events board. Walk has his paper up there. WHY DO WE STUDY HISTORY? the bulletin board asks.

"Why do we study history?" Hippie Sandals's blue eyes are straight on him.

"Otherwise you don't really understand the context of what's happening today." Walk can't help smiling at this. He knows he sounds good.

"I like the way you think," the man says. He seems satisfied and moves on.

"Who was that?" Matteo whispers.

"Beats me," Walk says.

Then Brianna shows up. Figures she'd come without an invitation. A guy in a suit that looks like it must have cost more than Sylvia's new 350 is walking with her.

Walk nods at her.

"Hi," Brianna says, glancing down quickly at Walk's project. "Oh, that one," she mutters, grabbing her father's arm and hurrying him along.

"Where is your work, Bree?" Brianna's father asks.

"Didn't put it out." She glances back at Walk. "I'm not the right color," she whispers. "I mean who are they going to ask . . . me . . . or some inner-city kid?"

Walk's stomach churns. His mouth tastes like dirt. If he does well they say, "He's black, they lowered the bar." He messes up and it's "I told ya so."

Walk kicks the table leg. But he can't get angry. Sylvia will kill him for that.

Now Sylvia is back in Balderis's face, asking him a million questions. Poor guy. He doesn't know what hit him. Then she heads for the bulletin board and gets all snagged up in a group of parents. "Excuse me," she says to Hippie Sandals. They both move left.

"Excuse me," Sandals says. They both move right.

"Excuse me." Sylvia's voice has an edge now. She plants her feet and Sandals moves around her.

85

When she gets over to Walk her eyes are fiery. She's breathing hard and clicking her nails against each other the way she does when she's upset. Walk's in no mood for this. "Why am *I* in trouble?" Walk asks her.

"You're not," she says.

"How come you're mad?"

"I'm not."

"You sure?" Walk asks.

"I'm sure," she says.

TWENTY-THREE

Kirsten

At lunch now I sit with Brianna, Rory, Madison, Lauren, and Maya. We take up an entire cafeteria table and pretty much all they do is talk about the talent show. Rory, Madison, and Brianna will be singing. Lauren and Maya will be dancing. They all stay after school to work with the professional director, who, according to Rory, Brianna's mom is paying for.

Lauren and Maya always sit next to each other. They look like twins from the back because all of their clothes have words across the butt. Maya has this dancer thing going. She walks as if every step is measured out in advance and she sits up extra straight, like slouching is beneath her. Lauren is tiny and she wears her hair like she thinks she's Cleopatra—Cleopatra with words across her butt. Then comes Madison, who half the time wears her gym clothes to school. She doesn't care. But Brianna would never say anything bad about Madison. Never.

I try to get here early because if I'm late Brianna puts her stuff on the extra seat, and I have to ask her to move it, like a complete and total loser. Of course, she apologizes the rest of lunch. But the way she says "sorry" every time she looks at me is even worse. Plus, then I'm sitting next to her all lunch, and that's risky because I haven't mastered the art of kissing her feet. I always trip on the way down.

Rory, on the other hand, is quite the foot kisser. She's so good, in fact, that I don't know when she's doing it and when she isn't. I thought I knew who Rory was, but maybe I was wrong. Maybe Rory never really liked me. Maybe she was just kissing *my* feet.

Today, I'm really trying hard to stay on my diet, but my lunch is so small, it's over in seconds. I think about all the snack food my mom has hidden in the garage. My mother is Costco-crazy. She finds these deals and buys in the tonnage, then forgets what's out there. There are enough of Kippy's potato chip bags to feed a starving country. She thinks I don't know about this.

"Oh my god, Brianna, you looked so good in that green dress," Lauren says.

Maya leans forward. "Yeah, and did you see Madison's brother checking you out last night?"

"He was not."

"Was too. He, like, had his eyes glued to your butt."

"You got together last night?" I whisper to Rory.

She shrugs. "We had rehearsal."

I work the plastic spoon under the tiny lip of the Yoplait to get the last little bit. The spoon slips and makes a scrapy plastic snap.

Brianna looks at me, pizza in hand. "Oh my god, I am so fat! Look at this, you guys." Brianna lifts up her shirt to show her perfectly flat, tanned stomach with a diamond-pierced navel. "Don't you think I'm fat? I'm going to have to lose ten pounds before the talent show."

Rory jumps in. "No, you look great."

"I'd give anything for a stomach like that," Lauren agrees.

"Me too," Maya says.

"Hey, want to work out tonight?" Madison suggests. "My dad just got a new ab cruncher."

"Wait," Brianna says. "I want to know what Kirsten thinks. Don't you think I'm fat, Kirsten?"

"No," I say, zipping up my lunch bag.

"I know. Let's see who's fatter. Kirsten, let's see your belly. Come on. Mine's fatter, I swear to god, Kirsten. Don't you swear, Rory?"

"Well, I, uh . . . ," Rory wheezes.

"Come on, Kirsten." Brianna looks around the crowded cafeteria. "No one's even looking. No one's going to see but us. And I'm going to lose. I swear I will."

"Brianna, cut it out," Madison whispers. "My mother will kill me if—"

"If what?" Brianna turns on her.

"You know." Madison rocks her head from side to side. At first I think she's standing up for me, but then I realize she just doesn't trust me not to tell my mother.

"Kirsten's not going to run home and tell her mommy, are you, Kirsten?" Brianna asks.

I want to leave, but I'm stuck to my seat. I look at the clock. Lunch is almost over. If only the bell will ring.

"I think Kirsten's *too thin*." Brianna can barely contain herself. "So here." She hands me the rest of her pizza and bursts out laughing. "Fatten up."

The pizza is in front of me. The cheese is all melty, just the way I like it. My stomach grumbles. I imagine sinking my teeth into it.

"Look, she's going to eat it," Brianna whispers.

I toss the pizza in the garbage can fast and pretend with all my heart that Brianna was wrong.

TWENTY-FOUR

Walk

Walk's just sitting here once again under the friendly neighborhood poster ONE WORLD: CULTURAL DIVERSITY AT MOUNTAIN. It's writers' notebook time.

Walker Jones
September 20

"If you don't like the way the world is, you have an obligation to change it. You just do it one step at a time."—Marian Wright Edelman

Everybody talks big about changes but mostly what they want you to do is keep your mouth shut. Don't say a word.

"There are right ways to make change," Sylvia says, "and wrong ways." But she doesn't mean it. Every step that looks to me like making a change looks to her like making trouble. I need somebody's

version of things besides Sylvia's tight-as-a-drum,
no-air way. I need to breathe.

When Walk looks up Brianna's elbow is on his desk. "Can I see?" she asks.

"Not a chance."

"I'll show you mine."

"Do whatever you want. But mine is mine. Not for you to see."

"Okay, be that way." She slides her elbow closer to Walk. "Oh, am I bothering you?" Her large brown eyes start that Bambi thing, and for a second Walk almost forgives her for dissing him, and for poisoning the food supply if she's done that, too.

"I would prefer you didn't lean on my desk," Walk says.

"You 'would prefer . . .' Oh, you are so cute." She bats her long eyelashes.

"Cut it out, Brianna."

"I didn't mean to bother you. I hope you believe me. Do you believe me?" She juts her chin out and cocks her head.

Walk does not shake his head yes or no.

"Know what? People think you're kind of cool . . . kind of, you know, *exotic*." She takes her elbow off his desk—his *exotic* desk.

Walk spends the rest of Ms. Scrushy's class wishing she'd put it back.

TWENTY-FIVE

Kirsten

When I get home my mom asks me twice how things are going with Rory and Brianna, Lauren, Madison, and Maya. It's as if she thinks I'm going to have a different answer at five than at eight. If she'd asked me this morning I might have, but now I just think: Get me away from them. All of them. I can just imagine what they're IMing each other now.

I'm on my way out of the garage with a Costco package of peanut butter crackers inside the sleeve of my sweater when my mom appears in the doorway with her tiny indoor pruning shears. My heart slips in my chest. She's going to ask me what I was doing in the garage.

"I know! Let's do a party here," she says.

"Mom! I don't want a party!"

The look in my mom's eyes tells me she's upset. She has heard something from Rebecca Dunkel.

"What?" I ask.

"It's really hard to be a lone wolf, Kirsten."

"I'm not a lone wolf."

"How about a slumber party? Wouldn't that be fun?"

I shake my head.

"Why don't you invite Rory over? Will you at least do that?"

I shake my head again—a very big, very sure shake.

"How about that Maya? Her family is so nice."

"I don't want to invite anyone over, okay?"

The corner of the crackers package pokes my wrist.

"There's always one they make fun of, Kirsten. There always is. You do not want to be that one."

"Mom, please." She's followed me into the kitchen. I grab an Evian.

"I want you to have fun, sweetie. You'll never be young like this again."

I snort. "Thank god."

"Sometimes you have to play the game, Kirsten. You don't want to be like Debby Decaterman. God, did the girls make fun of her. It was awful. But she kind of deserved it, too. She was pathetic."

"Pathetic. I know what that means. It means fat," I whisper.

My mother's face darkens. "I won't have you moping around here feeling sorry for yourself, making poor food choices." She slams the broom closet door. The dustpan crashes off the hook.

I walk up the back stairs. "Rory isn't my friend

anymore. None of the rest of them ever were," I say in a tiny voice, so tiny she can't hear.

When I get to history class the next morning I keep my head down. I don't even look at Rory or Brianna. I decorate my notebook with dark goth doodles while Balderis drones on and on about grades and points and projects. Then suddenly I hear him say, "Who wants to do an extra-credit project?"

Walk's hand shoots up, so does Matteo's—and then my arm goes up, too. I barely do *credit* projects much less *extra* credit, but my arm doesn't care. My arm wants a friend.

"Kirsten," Balderis calls.

I wasn't raising my hand. The words swirl around in my mouth but my lips stay locked.

Balderis smiles—a real smile—the first he has ever directed at me. Oh great. Now *he's* going to be disappointed in me, too. I need to wear a sign: DO NOT PIN YOUR HOPES ON ME. LETTING DOWN MY PARENTS IS A FULL-TIME JOB. I HAVE NO ENERGY LEFT TO DISAPPOINT ANYONE ELSE.

"Walk, Matteo, Sophia . . ." He hands each of us the extra-credit assignment.

"Think about this," Balderis says. "Make a choice. Then let me know your topic tomorrow."

Just because I raised my hand doesn't mean I'm actually going to do the assignment. What is he thinking?

Kirsten

"Sophia, you want to work with Matteo? Walk, how about you and Kirsten pairing up?"

I look down at the page. The title is in bold type: **Partner Current Events Project.**

"Sure," Walk says; he comes over to my desk. "Hey, Kirsten. You want to meet at the library after last period and we can get on this?"

Today? Who starts a project the first day?

"No, wait." He catches himself. "I got science study group today. How about tomorrow?"

"Tomorrow is good." I can manage to get cholera by tomorrow. Typhoid fever . . . West Nile virus. There's got to be at least one mosquito with West Nile virus flying around Mill Valley tonight.

Even so, I'm in a better mood the rest of the day.

TWENTY-SIX

Walk

The next day, Kirsten is in the library after school. She has the kind of face that looks like she should be out selling Girl Scout cookies. Wouldn't do well, though: somebody'd steal her cookies. No street smarts, that girl; wouldn't last ten minutes at City.

When Kirsten sees him, she smiles a big old needy smile. Walk takes a step back.

"Hey," he says.

"Hi," she says. She pulls back her chair, scraping the floor. Dorarian frowns at Walk. Walk smiles and waves. Dorarian does not smile. Matteo has Dorarian all wrapped up in a little box tied with a bow, but Walk hasn't made a bit of progress with her, yet.

"I read it," Kirsten says, her blue eyes big.

"What?"

"The assignment."

She wants a gold star for *reading* the assignment? "Yeah, okay . . . You get a newspaper?"

"Oh." She nods, like Walk just gave her something really complicated to do. She doesn't move.

"What?" Walk asks.

"I didn't do it, you know. Steal Balderis's wallet. Brianna admitted she did it."

"Never thought you did."

She nods. "Yeah, thanks, you know, for that."

"But can I ask you something?" Walk taps his pencil against the table. "Why do you hang with her?"

"Who?"

"Brianna."

"I have lots of . . . I sit with lots of people." She tosses her hair over her shoulder. "Rory, Madison . . ."

Walk snorts. "Your momma never taught you to stay away from snakes?"

"What's that supposed to mean?"

"Somebody treat me the way Brianna and Rory treat you, I wouldn't go eating lunch with them."

Her lip gets shaky; she starts breathing fast. *Oh no. . . . She's going to cry.*

"Listen," Walk blurts out, "we eat at the back corner table, then we head down to the library. You can sit with us."

Walk can't believe he just said this. What is his problem? *You a fool*, he tells himself.

But the girl is smiling so big, he can't take it back now.

TWENTY-SEVEN

Kirsten

At the cafeteria the next day, I head for Walk's table. My head is busy planning what to say. *Can I sit with you guys today?* Dumb. *How about hi? Hi is good. Everybody says hi.*

But no one's sitting at Walk's table. Oh great. What am I going to do now? Rory's sitting with Maya and Lauren. Madison and Brianna aren't there yet. I don't want to sit with them, but who else am I going to sit with? Maybe if I eat fast, I can get out of there before Brianna shows up.

"Kirsten?" Rory smiles like the old Rory. Without thinking I sit down next to her like she's still my friend.

Brianna's seat is empty, just waiting for her to arrive. No one would dare put their stuff on the Queen's seat; it's permanently reserved for her.

I'm just about ready to get out of there when suddenly she and Madison show up. Brianna slams her books down, sending Rory's chips flying.

"I can't even believe it. I totally, totally can't believe it," Brianna says.

"What?" Maya asks.

"I got a fail test notice from Balderis for the test last Friday, but I *didn't* fail. I got a C."

Maya shrugs her narrow shoulders. "It's a mistake."

"I just spent the last half hour talking to him. Turns out he's taking off two hundred points for bad behavior—that's what he called it—because of the day we were playing around with his wallet."

The wallet. I shift position on the round saucer seat, which is built for a bikini-size butt, not one the size of mine.

"I worked it out with Fishhouse," Brianna continues. "It's totally not fair for Balderis to dock my grade now. It is so wrong. So, so wrong. I got a C!"

Everyone is looking at her. I don't know whether to look or not look.

"Bet anything you're going to get one, too," Brianna tells Rory.

"I got a B plus on Balderis's test," Rory whispers.

"Minus two hundred points is an F," Brianna tells her. "It wasn't even a regular school day. We were, like, helping him. How can he take off for that? It's so totally bogus."

"We can't fail," Rory says, "or they won't let us in the talent show."

Lauren tosses her Cleopatra hair. "Go talk to Fishhouse," she says.

"Yeah," Madison agrees.

"I will. Maybe we both should?" Brianna looks at Rory.

Rory stares at the pocket of her backpack where she always keeps her inhaler. Her nostrils are flaring like she really needs it, but it makes her look weird, so she doesn't get it out. Better to die than that.

"At least you don't have Dolman," Brianna tells Rory. "Practically everyone fails at least one test from Dolman."

Rory says nothing.

Brianna looks around. "What's *your* problem?" she suddenly asks me.

"Nothing," I say. *I'm just sitting here perfecting the totally blank look. Blank Looks "R" Us.*

"I expect you to help me with this, too, you know."

"Me . . . I . . . *me?*"

"I could have let you take the rap and then I wouldn't be in trouble. But I didn't. I got you out of it."

"Yeah, but . . . but . . ."

"I try really hard to be a *nice* person and look out for my friends. We are *friends*, right?" Brianna asks, her voice soft, her mouth open, her eyes totally sincere.

Is she kidding me? After yesterday?

She stares at me so intensely it feels like there is no one in the cafeteria but her and me.

"What do you want from me?" I whisper, or maybe I just think I say this. Maybe I say nothing.

101

Kirsten

"Oh come on, Kirsten, don't look so worried," she says. "I really like you, you know. I really do."

I have to get out of here.

She seems to already know this. She picks up my backpack and hands it to me and I start walking.

I glance back at her expecting her to be mad, but her face is shining. She's waving her hand.

I smile back. I can't help myself.

Then I see she's waving to a dark-haired eighth grader who is the cutest guy in the whole school.

TWENTY-EIGHT

Walk

Walk doesn't see Kirsten at lunch for a day or two. He figures she isn't going to take him up on his offer. But then on Monday she's headed for his lunch table. Of course it was too much to hope she'd turn him down. "Yo, Kirsten." Walk makes room for her.

Kirsten smiles and giggles. "Hi." She kicks her legs over the seat.

"Hi," Matteo says.

Hair Boy and Jade just stare.

"Do you have candy?" Jade asks.

"I wish," Kirsten says. "The office lady does, though. Sometimes she'll give you a piece."

"Not here today," Jade answers. "And neither is her candy."

Jade's a candy-head. Her lunch bag looks like she's been out trick-or-treating with it. No sandwich, no fruit, no chips, just candy, only today she forgot her bag.

"Hey, how many bathrooms you have?" Walk asks.

"Me?" Kirsten shifts on her seat.

"We've been talking about how rich people have a lot of bathrooms," Walk explains.

"Way more than the number of butts in the house," Jade says. "Seems like there ought to be a law against having more bathrooms than you have butts."

"A butt law?" Kirsten asks.

"Buttocks Law: a special section of the penal code," Walk says.

"Penal code?" Matteo cracks up.

"What's the most bathrooms you've ever personally seen in one house?" Hair Boy wants to know.

"Five," Jade says.

"I've seen seven," Matteo answers.

"Ten," Kirsten blurts out.

"Ten? If you have ten bathrooms, how do you decide which one to use? Are they color coded?" Walk asks.

"Maybe you pee blue in the blue bathroom and taupe in the taupe bathroom," Kirsten suggests.

"What color do you pee if it's wallpaper with a pattern?" Jade asks.

"Good question," Kirsten answers.

"No, really. How many bathrooms do you have?" Jade's weird green eyes focus on Kirsten.

"Three and a half," Kirsten says.

"A half a bathroom. What is that?" Walk asks.

"Just for one cheek," Kirsten explains.

"What you do with the other cheek?" Jade wants to know.

"Strictly for show," Kirsten answers.

"Can't turn the other cheek if you only have one," Matteo offers.

"But there are problems with one-cheek butts," Kirsten says, her face all serious now. "You have to get your pants tailor-made, go online to buy special chairs."

"Are there support groups?" Jade asks.

"Yes," Kirsten says. "And a website, onecheekbuttocksdotcom, for all your one-cheek accessories."

By the time Dorarian appears with her blue fur thermos, everyone is cracking up. Then they all start walking to the library, like Kirsten's been hanging with them for weeks. This is so weird.

"You guys done with Balderis's extra credit?" Matteo asks.

"Just putting the finishing touches, buffing it all up, man," Walk tells him.

Matteo looks at Walk then Kirsten. "You're not done, are you?"

Walk gives him an ugly look. "Shaddup," he says.

"What did you pick?" Matteo asks.

"Cloning," Walk tells him. "I'm for it because the world needs more MLKs, JFKs, and Boutros Boutros-Ghalis."

"Boutros Boutros-Ghali? Who is he? She? Them?" Kirsten asks.

Walk

"Him. It's one guy. He ran the United Nations," Walk tells her.

"Really? Boutros Boutros-Ghali like I could be Kirsten Kirsten-McKenna?"

"Hair Hair-Boy," Hair Boy says.

Jade flips her skateboard over. She taps her leg like she's calling her dog. "Here, here boy."

"Shut up," Hair Boy says, jumping on his skateboard and tearing after her.

In the library, Walk pulls Kirsten aside. "Hey, you gotta finish your extra credit this weekend, okay?"

"I thought we were done?" Kirsten says.

"No, we're not done!" Walk shouts at her.

"It was a joke, Walker Walker. I'll get it finished, okay?"

When the bell rings, Matteo and Walk head to the gym.

"Good call," Matteo tells Walk.

"What?" Walk asks.

"Inviting Kirsten."

"Oh, that. Sure. I knew all along she was our kind. I got an instinct for people. You just sit back and watch, man, just sit back and watch."

106

TWENTY-NINE

Kirsten

I'm emailing Walk. He doesn't have IM, plus he shares a computer with his mom so I can't write any weird jokes. "No butt jokes" is what he said. At least he has email. Matteo doesn't have email or a computer or anything. Who doesn't have a computer except for maybe if you're Amish?

"Kirsten?" My mom comes into my room with her bowl of air-popper popcorn. "Are you busy?"

"Sort of."

"What are you doing?"

I look up at her. She is trying to read the screen, which so far only says, *I am so*

"Who are you emailing?" She pops a piece of popcorn into her mouth.

"A friend."

"You know, that's what I wanted to talk to you about. Rebecca Dunkel called me this afternoon. She told me something I'm"—she sucks in her breath—"a little concerned about."

"What?"

"She says that you don't sit with the girls anymore. You sit with the boys. And everyone wonders why."

"Oh, that. Don't worry, Mom. Things are fine." I turn back to my computer.

"But I *am* worried. What are you doing with these boys, Kirsten?"

My head snaps back. "Oh god, Mom. They're my friends. It's not like that. It isn't."

She looks hard at me, her mouth chewing tiny bites one hundred miles an hour.

"Okay, okay. I thought that's what you'd say. But you know reputations are a delicate thing, Kirsten. Once you get a bad reputation, it can stay with you all the way through high school."

"Yeah, but it's a lie."

"Even if it is a lie."

"So what am I supposed to do? I can't keep people from lying."

"Look"—she sets down her bowl—"I think what's happened is Rory and Brianna and Madison feel a little rejected by you."

"By me? Hello? *By me?*"

"Yes. That's what I think. And their feelings are hurt. So maybe if you ate lunch with them sometimes. Because, you know, it isn't natural for seventh-grade girls to always eat lunch with boys, unless . . ." She jiggles her popcorn. The unpopped old maids rattle on the bottom.

"Mom, you got this wrong. That's *so* not what's happening. You gotta trust me on this, okay?"

She looks at me. "These are nice boys?"

"Mom . . . I'm doing extra-credit assignments because *of them*. These are the nicest boys."

"Even so, Kirsten . . ."

"Besides, there's another girl who sits with us, too. Her name is Jade."

"Jade? Jade Schwartz? The girl who wears army clothes to school every day?"

"Not every day."

My mother groans. She definitely won't like Jade. Will she like Walk and Matteo?

Matteo is so polite. And everybody loves Walk. If she could just get to know Walk and Matteo, she wouldn't worry. "Mom, look, I'll bring them home, okay? Because it's *so* not the way Rebecca Dunkel says. If you could meet them, I know you'd see."

She bites her lip. "You'll let me meet them?"

"Of course."

"And they're nice?"

"I promise," I say, though suddenly I remember how weird she was about Walk that first day, but it was only because she wanted to meet his mom, right?

I go back to my computer but I can feel she is still standing at the door.

Kirsten

"Kirsten, tell me you're not going to start wearing army fatigues every day?"

I jump up and give her a hug. "I promise I won't, Mom. Okay? I promise."

THIRTY

Walk

Pleeeeease!" Kirsten pleads. Walk hates to see girls beg, but he really doesn't want to come over to her house just because Kirsten's mom wants to make sure he isn't a bad boy.

"How about Matteo?" he says. "Couldn't you ask him?"

"He has to help his dad with something."

"Yeah, and I have student council."

"You can come over after. Pleeeeease. She just wants to see that you're nice."

"I'm not nice."

"Yes you are."

"No I'm not."

She rolls her eyes.

"What am I supposed to do? Say the pledge of allegiance, the ten commandments? How far is it, anyway?"

"It's only a mile. Come on. We can finish the extra credit and you can check out our bathrooms! And I will owe you, like, forever for this." She shoves her cell in his face.

"Forever?"

"Forever."

Walk can see she's not going to let up on this. "Oh, man," he mutters, taking her cell. He leaves a message for Sylvia to pick him up at five at Kirsten McKenna's house. Walk tells her how to get there, even though Sylvia always knows how to get everywhere. She has a GPS wired in her brain.

"Why am I doing this?" Walk hands Kirsten's cell back.

"Because you like me."

"I do?"

"Yes," she tells him.

When Walk gets out of student council and heads for Kirsten's house he wishes more than ever he'd told her no. She lives in the heart of white world. All the houses are enormous, as if somebody shot them full of steroids. Kirsten's house is brand-new. It looks as if the path was swept fifteen minutes ago. Even the dirt on the ground isn't dirty; it's hidden under these bark chip things. The place is all decked out like one of those poor circus dogs wearing a matching hat and jacket.

The doorbell chimes a few bars of Bob Dylan. The door cracks open and a little girl, who looks like a tiny Kirsten—Kirsten put in the dryer and shrunk all up—sticks her head out. "Who are you?" she asks.

"Walker Jones, Kirsten's friend."

"Are you a *nice* friend or a *mean* friend?" she asks, her shrunken Kirsten eyes gone all squinty.

"I don't think you can be a *mean friend*," Walk answers.

"Oh, yes you can. Kirsten has lots of mean friends."

Walk laughs. "I guess she does."

"She's my best sister," the little girl says, her face all fierce. She looks Walk up and down.

Mini Kirsten is tougher than the super-sized one. Mini Kirsten knows how to push back. Walk raises his hand like he's taking an oath. "I'll be nice," he says.

"Do you like rabbits?"

"Yes, very much." Walk tries hard to keep a straight face.

Her mouth curls to one side like she's thinking about this. "Okay." She opens the door. "You can come in."

"Hey, Walk." Kirsten comes down a big staircase. The little girl turns to Kirsten and whispers, "I checked him out. He's okay."

"Nice work," Kirsten says. "That's my little sister, Kippy."

"Hi," Kippy says to Walk, then she whispers to Kirsten, "Mom wants you in the craft room."

The craft room? What is this, the YMCA?

They go to the kitchen. At least Walk thinks it's the kitchen. There are three sinks. "One sink, two sink, red sink, blue sink," Walk says.

Kirsten looks like she never counted how many sinks she has in her own kitchen.

"Okay, I give up. Where's the refrigerator?" Walk asks.

Kirsten yanks on a large white wood cabinet. Inside the refrigerator is big enough to hold bodies. Bathroom like this, too? Gigantic toilets that sink into the floor?

But it's the living room that busts Walk's eyes out of his head. Big windows looking out at the whole of San Francisco across the Bay.

"Whoa," Walk says.

Kirsten smiles. "Nice, huh?"

Walk snorts. "You could give tours of this place."

In "the craft room" they sit in wicker chairs at a wicker table with wicker baskets—each labeled SCISSORS, BEADS, MARKERS. *This is kindergarten,* Walk thinks. Any minute they'll crank up the *Barney* song and a purple dinosaur will come in and shake his hand.

"You bet. Let's talk tonight." A fine-looking woman with long white-blond hair and tight jeans walks in. She flips closed her cell.

"I'm Walk." Walk reaches out his hand.

Mrs. McKenna stares at him like he has burrito dribbled down his shirt. Her hand is cold in his.

"You have a beautiful house, Mrs. McKenna. Thanks so much for inviting me over." Walk lays it on thick. That's why he's here, right?

114

"Uh, thank you." Mrs. McKenna's eyes zip from Walk to Kirsten and back. "You're in the same class, you two?"

"History," Kirsten says. "Walk and Matteo have more points than anyone in the whole class, Mom."

"Points?" Mrs. McKenna asks.

"It means they're the head of the class, Mom. Really smart."

"Oh. That's nice. Well, I see you're working," she says like she can't get out of there fast enough.

Walk looks at Kirsten. "Not much of a third degree."

Kirsten shrugs. "One look at you was all she needed."

"You tell her something about me?"

"That you're nice. She'll come back and ask more. My mom's gotta know everything. She leaves the door open when she pees so she won't miss out on the conversation while she's in the bathroom."

"Remind me not to walk by the bathroom."

"This is our favorite subject, you know."

"Hey, don't look at me. I'm not the one brought it up."

While they're doing homework, Kippy brings them dinky cups of nasty-looking green juice that she claims is just pineapple juice plus a secret ingredient, but it smells strange, like boiled spinach water. Then

115

she needs help with a word in *Fifty Ways to Make Ooze*, and after that she asks, "When is it going to be time to feed the bunnies?"

Then Kirsten's father shows up. Guess the whole family has to check Walk out. The guy kind of looks like his wife. Blond handsome with blond bushy eyebrows, a square jaw, and small round glasses. He's tall and lean like a tennis player and he walks like he knows he looks good even in his scrubs. Wait. He looks familiar. It's the hippie-sandals guy, only he's in real shoes now.

"Dad," Kirsten says. "What are you doing home?"

"I'm on my way to the hospital. Thought I'd stop by for a minute."

"Oh, okay, well, this is Walk."

"We've met," Walk says, taking Mr. McKenna's outstretched hand. "At the Open House."

"That's right. Nice to see you again." He shakes Walk's hand.

"Daddy!" Kippy pops in. "Look! I've read all the way to page fifty-three today!"

"Very good, Kip." He messes up her hair. "My little chemist."

"Yep, we're going to call her Doctor Goop," Kirsten mutters.

"So Walk"—Mr. McKenna pulls up a chair—"how do you like school? What's your best subject?"

"History."

"How are you in science? Got any aptitude there?"

"I'm okay," Walk says.

Mr. McKenna nods like he wants more.

"I got an A in science, but I like history and English better," Walk tells him.

"What's your GPA, if you don't mind me asking?"

"Dad!" Kirsten growls.

"4.0," Walk says.

Mr. McKenna takes off his glasses and polishes them all up with a little blue rag he has in his pocket. "I understand you have to do better than 4.0 to get into Cal," he tells his glasses.

"Cal?" Walk asks.

"UC Berkeley," Mr. McKenna says.

"They don't offer AP classes until ninth grade," Walk tells him.

"So 4.0 is as good as it gets right now?" Mr. McKenna asks.

"Yes, sir," Walk says.

Mr. McKenna smiles so big it looks like it might split his face apart. "Well, I gotta get going. It's good to meet you, Walk."

When he's gone, Kirsten stares at Walk. "You really have a 4.0?"

Walk shrugs. "They don't give out scholarships for nothing, you know."

"You definitely passed with my dad. That's for sure."

Walk rolls his eyes at her. "Of course I did."

"Tell me something . . . Do you ever doubt yourself, *ever*?" she asks.

"No," Walk tells her. "Never."

THIRTY-ONE

Kirsten

"So, you feel better now, Mom?" I ask. She's been in bed since Walk left.

"I have a migraine, Kirsten. There is no feeling better."

"A migraine? You've never had a migraine before."

My mom doesn't move. She is lying on her bed with a washcloth on her head.

"I'm sorry, Mom. I was just wondering if you liked Walk?"

"Seems nice enough. My head is killing me, honey. Could you get some dinner for you and Kippy? I can't talk right now."

"Sure, Mom. Can I get you something? Advil or anything?"

"That would be nice, babe. I'll take four."

THIRTY-TWO

Walk

At ten minutes to five Walk heads for the street to wait for Sylvia, but she's there already, parked down the block like she got the wrong address.

The car door's open, Sylvia's leg is kicked out, and smoke curls out of a cigarette in her hand. When she sees Walk, she drops the cigarette, grinds it out, and shuts the door.

Walk knocks on the window and she rolls it down. "I can't believe you," he says.

"You getting in?" she asks, searching through her CDs.

"Momma! What's the matter with you?"

"I'm not gonna start smoking again, if that's what you're worried about," she announces when Walk clicks his seat belt.

"What happened to 'One cigarette is too many, a million aren't enough'? What happened to that?"

"I had a slip, okay? Let's not blow this out of proportion. Nobody got lung cancer from one cigarette.

Here." She hands Walk the pack. "You can throw them away."

When they get to a gas station, Walk finds a trash can, punches the package past a mess of Styrofoam cups all the way to the bottom.

Back in the 350, Walk slams the door again. "Why?" he asks.

She pops in Charlie Parker, pops it out. Slides in Fats Waller, takes him out. "I made a mistake. Can we leave it at that?"

"No."

She groans. "Shall we get a pizza on the way home?"

"Yes."

"So what did you do at Kirsten's?"

"Homework."

"Anything else?"

"What's that supposed to mean?"

"Nothing. I was just wondering what you were doing . . ."

"I just told you: homework."

"Yeah, you did. Whatever happened with the wallet?"

"Kirsten didn't take it. Some girl named Brianna set her up."

Sylvia takes a deep breath. "So you and Kirsten are . . . friends now?"

"Is that what you're upset about? You think she's my girlfriend?"

"No." She sighs, her hand fixes her hair, touches the cigarette lighter. "I had an awful day at work, Walk. This doesn't have anything to do with you."

"You sure?"

"Yes," she says softly, "I'm sure."

Walk

THIRTY-THREE

Kirsten

When I get up the next morning, my mom is still asleep, but my father's side of the bed looks untouched, like he slept on the couch. Downstairs, Kippy is busy reading *Tree Doctor: A Complete Guide to Tree Care and Maintenance.*

"Did you see the new tree Dad bought?" Kip asks.

"Is he here?"

"Yeah. Look, he got me this book. He said I can be in charge of watering, pruning, fertilizer . . ." Kip follows me to our dad's office, still holding the book.

My father looks up from his laptop. "Well, if it isn't my two brilliant daughters." He puts his arms out to us.

"One brilliant daughter, Dad," I mutter.

"Tell her about the tree! Tell her," Kip says.

"I bought a tree for out front. A new tree. A new beginning. Won't that be nice? Everything is going to be fine here. Yes it is," my father says.

"Yay!" Kippy yells at the top of her lungs.

I wish I could believe him the way she does, but at least he's trying. I even think about showing him my extra credit. Well, for a nanosecond, anyway. I did a good job on that extra credit. That was more work than I usually do all year. But when I showed it to Walk, he was like: "Yeah, fine, turn it in." *Yeah, fine, turn it in.* Excuse me? That was all weekend working my butt off.

I'd better get full points, that's all I can say, because that work is great. More than great. Stupendous, in fact. Now I need a spa day.

When I get to class and see Balderis writing EXTRA CREDIT on the board, I say to myself, *Not me.* Not this week. Besides, Walk isn't even here.

Matteo smiles at me. I look around to see if he's smiling at someone else. He isn't.

"Hey," he whispers. "You want to work together this week? Walk's got some big student council thing."

"Sure." I raise my hand, looking over at Rory. See this, Rory? I've got friends. I don't need you.

But Rory and Brianna have their hands up, too. It's amazing what they'll do to stay in that talent show. Rory is wearing makeup and she's got new clothes. They're tighter, with a lot more skin showing—the kind of clothes fat girls can't wear. When she sits down, you can see her butt crack. She's even given up the backpack she used to carry. It had a tiny unicorn stitched on the

123

Kirsten

front. She never could decide what to name the unicorn. Every day it was something different. Now she has a blue backpack. It could be anybody's.

"All right, I'll let you pick your own partners this week," Balderis says. "One hundred possible points, same as before." Balderis raises a stack of pages in the air.

"Brianna," Balderis calls.

"Can I work with Matteo?" Brianna asks.

Why would Brianna pick him? Must be she needs an A and she knows Matteo will get her one.

"Brianna and Matteo." Balderis writes them down.

Matteo's face caves. He says nothing, but I can hear him dying two seats away.

"Sophia," Balderis calls.

"Tessa," Sophia says.

"Rory," Balderis says.

"Kirsten," Rory says.

Rory picked me?

Brianna picked Matteo. That is the only reason Rory picked me, I remind myself, but I can't help smiling at her as she slides into the seat next to mine.

"Um, when do you want to meet to work on this?" I ask.

"You could come to my house and then have dinner over." Her eyes are big and innocent like she's my stuffed puppy.

I think about all the sleepovers we did. The day we wrapped each other in toilet paper and pretended to be mummies. The time we went to the beach and a dog stole Rory's shoe and buried it under a dead fish. The Halloween we decided to dress as salt and pepper shakers and fought over who got to be salt and who got to be pepper.

"It's better to work in the library," I say. "They have all the newspapers and stuff."

"The library?" she asks as if I've just suggested we do our homework on the freeway divider.

I shrug.

"We can still be friends, you know, even if I'm friends with them," Rory says.

Oh great, she'll be friends with me when they aren't around. I'm the spare.

But I can't deny the warmth coming from her.

"You've, like, forgiven me, haven't you?" she asks.

"Sure," I say, trying to sound as if I haven't given it much thought one way or the other.

"I was just wondering because . . . Where have you been sitting at lunch? I thought I saw you with the"— her voice drops to a whisper—"poor kids."

"The poor kids?" I ask.

"Yeah, *you know.*"

I shake my head.

"Okay, well, whatever. I just miss you. That's all I'm trying to say."

"Are you and Madison doing a lot of sleepovers and stuff?" I can't keep myself from asking this.

"Some. She has, you know, *other friends,* too."

Kirsten

Is this code for Madison is dumping her? Poor Rory. She's really nice. Well, she used to be nice, anyway. Who knows who she is now.

"What do you mean?" I ask.

"Nothing, I'm just saying. We had fun, didn't we?" She kicks at her new could-be-anyone's backpack. "Hey, how are your parents, you know, getting along?"

I look at the backpack, the new pants, the new makeup. This is not the same Rory.

"Fine," I say as the bell rings and I zip up my binder. "Never better."

THIRTY-FOUR

Walk

Walker Jones
October 5

"All human beings should strive to learn before they die what they are running from, and to, and why."—James Thurber

What's this Thurber guy's problem? Who does he think he is? I'm not running from anything or anyone, and nobody I know is running from or to or around in circles, either. I've got better things to do, okay?

Sorry, Ms. Scrushy. I'm doing my best here, but this guy is dead wrong about this.

The elbow is back.

"What do you want?" Walk asks.

Brianna cocks her head. "Oh, is this bothering you?"

"What do you think?"

"Do you have Dolman?"

"No."

"Lucky you. Matteo does though, right?"

"Uh-huh."

"Matteo is like a math genius, isn't he?"

Walk shrugs. "More or less."

"*Yes!*" She pumps her fist in the air. "That's what I thought."

The way she says this bugs Walk. He puts his elbow on *her* desk now.

"What's the deal with you and Matteo?" Walk stares her down.

"The deal?"

"You pick on him. You act like you own the air he breathes."

"What are you talking about? I just said he was a math genius. And besides, I don't pick on anyone. I am very kind to everyone. He's the one acts all weird about it."

"About what?"

She raises her eyebrows. "He never told you?"

"Told me *what?*"

She scoffs. "I thought you were friends."

"Told me what?" Walk demands.

"Hello? About his mom!"

"What about his mom?"

"She's our maid. She, like, cleans my house. Scrub-a-dub-dub," Brianna sings.

"Liar."

She snorts. "Oh yeah? You ask him."

But Walk doesn't have to ask him. He can tell by her stupid smug face it's true.

So that's what's going on.

Walk

THIRTY-FIVE

Kirsten

At lunch I head for the library table where Matteo and Walk usually sit. Matteo's backpack hangs on his chair, but it's Brianna's voice I hear. Brianna in the library? Now that's unusual.

"Brianna!" Matteo calls. "Come on."

Brianna snorts, then suddenly appears from behind the stacks. She glares at me. "What are you looking at?" she asks as she sails out the door.

Matteo sits down. His face looks like a crumpled paper bag.

"What was that all about?"

He shoves his highlighter pack into his backpack, and gets up.

"Hey, wait up," I call, hurrying after him, but just as I get to the door of the library, Dorarian appears, blocking my way.

"Everything okay?" Dorarian squints, pressing her glasses up her nose.

"Yeah, sure, uh-huh." I push past her just as Matteo ducks into the school office.

I hurry after him. He's headed for the outside door.

"Excuse me." The office secretary comes up behind him. She is wearing purple pants, purple sweater, purple shirt, and purple jewelry—all of it large.

"Oh hi," I call to her, waving my Kippy-ish wave, up around my ear.

"You two are not allowed back here," she barks.

"I'm sorry. I'm starving," I whisper. "My mom has me on Atkins. I swear to god I could eat a house. Matteo was just keeping me company."

"Oh." She looks at me, then Matteo. Her big face softens. "I tried Atkins. I would have killed for a banana. And then you're supposed to eat fried pork rinds? It's disgusting.

"Next time, ask first," she tells me, taking the cover off her purple candy dish.

"Thank you! I really appreciate this," I tell her.

Back out in the hall, Matteo smiles at me.

"Now will you tell me what's going on?" I ask.

Walk's head pops up from the water fountain. He wipes his mouth. "Yeah, what *is* going on?"

"Brianna wants to copy my Dolman take-home," Matteo tells us.

"You're kidding," I say.

"You get caught, you'll lose your scholarship," Walk says.

131

Kirsten

"You think I don't know that?" Matteo whispers.

Walk nods his head. "You're not gonna do it, right?"

"Why would he do it?" I say. "It's crazy."

Matteo's nostrils flare.

I look at Walk then Matteo. "What? What am I missing?"

"His mom works for Brianna's mom," Walk explains.

Matteo gives Walk a sharp look. "How'd you know?" he mutters.

"I know everything," Walk says. "What happens if you say no?"

"Brianna makes trouble for my mom," Matteo tells the floor.

"What kind of trouble?" I ask.

"Accuses her of things. Breaking glasses, plates, platters, stealing . . . She comes home and cries and cries."

My mouth drops open. I shut it again. Matteo's mom is the *cleaning lady*? I think about Bonita, our cleaning lady. I hope they don't know we have a cleaning lady. All cleaning ladies don't know one another, right? Of course they don't.

"This time she said she'd say my mom stole." Matteo's voice is so low it's hard to hear him.

"If you don't give her the test?" I ask.

He nods.

"Whoa." Walk sucks his breath in.

"She can't do that," I say.

"Sure she can," Matteo says.

"We can't let her," I say.

Matteo won't look at me.

"But it's not right," I whisper. "It's just not."

Kirsten

THIRTY-SIX

Walk

Hey, man, you can't keep doing whatever she wants," Walk tells Matteo when they're changing into their gym clothes.

Matteo slams his gym locker. "I don't do whatever she wants."

"What do you call it, then?"

"I call it none of your business, Walk."

"I'm your friend, man. Don't you know that?"

Matteo ties his shoes slowly, methodically, like it requires all his attention to get the bow just so. Walk waits for him to answer. He doesn't.

"Does your mom know about this?"

Matteo pulls his shirtsleeves over his bulging arms. "My mom thinks you should believe the best of people. Brianna is a nice girl." He imitates a heavy Spanish accent. "'Maybe your English not good, *mijo*. Maybe you don't understand.'"

"How does she figure you get straight As, man?"

Matteo shrugs.

"How about your dad?"

"He doesn't even think I should be at this school."

"Why?"

Matteo twirls the dial on his gym locker. "He thinks I'm going to forget who I am."

"When's Dolman's take-home due?"

"Third period tomorrow."

"Doesn't give you a lot of time."

"No kidding."

"So what are you gonna do?"

Matteo glares at him.

"Okay, okay." Walk raises his palms up. "I'll back off. I will."

Walk

THIRTY-SEVEN

Kirsten

When I call Walk he says: "I told Matteo I'd back off. He doesn't want help."

"You sure?"

"I'm sure," he says.

"Really sure?"

"Really sure."

But after I hang up, I can't stop thinking about Matteo. Brianna can't do this. She just can't. Walk was right. She really is a snake—a boa that hugs you to death.

When I fall asleep, I dream of unicorns. Hundreds and hundreds of unicorns, each one asking, "What is my name?"

I wake up and decide I should talk to Rory. I don't know what I'll say exactly, but I can't leave this alone. I have to find out what she knows.

Rory's dad doesn't drive her all the way to the drop-off because he's always in a rush to get to work. He lets her out at the corner by the gas station and she walks from there. I don't have to wait long before Rory's dad's silver Lexus pulls up.

"Rory," I say as she gets out.

Rory checks to make sure no one else is here. I can't imagine Brianna or Madison ever meeting her at the gas station, but it still hurts. "Oh hi, Kirsten," she says when she's satisfied no one is around to see her talking to me.

"You and Brianna and Madison doing the talent show next week?"

"Yeah, if they let us."

"Why wouldn't they let you? You guys are doing the extra credit for Balderis."

"Brianna got a fail notice in Dolman's. She has to get an A on the take-home or she's sunk."

"Dolman's hard. I'm glad I didn't get her," I say as we start walking to school.

"Me too," she agrees.

"Matteo has been working like *crazy* on that take-home. And you know how smart he is."

"Wait. You aren't *really* friends with Matteo, are you? Do you know his mom is like a maid?" She coughs. Her voice gets high and wheezy.

I get her inhaler out of her backpack and hand it to her.

"Yep. Matteo's my friend," I say after she's taken a puff.

"*Boyfriend?*"

137

Kirsten

"No. Look, I might be able to help with the Dolman take-home."

I'm not exactly sure where I'm going with this. I don't want to get in the middle because if it blows up, Matteo and Walk will hate me. Walk told me not to get involved. I should just back off, but a plan is taking shape.

Rory's eyes key in on me. "Really?" she asks.

"Uh-huh," I say, "but this would be just, you know, for you. Not for Brianna, all right?"

"Brianna and I are just friends at school and stuff. You and I are best friends forever—"

"Sure." I cut her off and take a deep breath. "I saw Matteo put his Dolman take-home in his backpack. The front pocket. He has this, you know, Velcro organizer thing. It's, like, green and he keeps his highlighters in there and his money and stuff. The take-home's in there."

She nods. "Really? Oh. Thanks . . . like, really, thanks! Come by at lunch, okay? I miss you." She smiles the old Rory smile.

Next thing I do is pay a visit to Dorarian the librarian.

"Dorarian," I tell her, "you have to do me a favor."

"And why is that?" she asks, looking at me over the top of her sparkly blue glasses.

"Because it's really for Matteo."

"Matteo?" She stops marking books and looks at me.

"Call Matteo out of Balderis's first period because he has an overdue library book. But it has to be right before the end of class. Like nine twenty-five."

"Matteo would never have an overdue library book," Dorarian informs me.

"You'll be wrong," I tell her.

"I'm never wrong."

"This time you will be."

"You want to tell me what you're up to, young lady?"

"I can't. You have to trust me."

"Why should I?"

"Because I'm doing the right thing."

She takes off her glasses and starts chewing on them. "I suppose it couldn't hurt to think Matteo has an overdue library book and be *mistaken*."

"Yes! Thank you!" My arms fly out like I'm going to hug her.

She puts her hands up like I shouldn't come near.

I can't help laughing at this. I don't know why. "Nine twenty-five, okay?" I tell her, half running down the hall.

I'm late when I get back to Balderis's class.

Balderis raps his knuckles on the table. "Ms. Mc-Kenna, I thought we were over the tardiness problem."

"Sorry," I mumble, hurrying to my seat.

139

Balderis makes a big theatrical sigh as he writes me a pinky. "Take it to the office after class. I don't want you to miss any of the lecture," he says, and continues on with his explanation.

Walk looks at me. His eyes ask what I'm up to. What if I blow this?

Brianna and Rory are giggling and whispering, watching me. When they see me look at them, they quick change to their pretend smiles and wave. I wave back, then I write a note to Matteo. PUT YOUR TAKE-HOME IN YOUR HIGHLIGHTER PACK IN THE FRONT COMPARTMENT OF YOUR BACKPACK. THAT IS ALL YOU HAVE TO DO. I SWEAR, SWEAR, DOUBLE SWEAR.

He shakes his head a tiny fierce no.

I write him another note. TRUST ME.

He glares at me, but he unzips the front pocket of his backpack and starts digging in it.

Then I write a note to Balderis. BRIANNA HAS STOLEN MATTEO'S HIGHLIGHTER PACK WITH HIS MONEY IN IT.—ANONYMOUS

Now I have to wait and just hope. What a crappy plan. Too many things have to happen for this to work. What was I thinking?

Balderis lectures until 9:15, then he takes questions until 9:20. I draw one hangman, but I can't finish. I'm too nervous to draw.

"Okay, extra-credit groups, five minutes to get your act together," Balderis announces at 9:20.

But Brianna is across the room from Matteo.

140

What's she doing way over there? She has to move closer. I get together with Rory and keep my eyes peeled for Dorarian. This is never going to work. I may as well kill myself now.

The clock ticks 9:22. Rory is telling me about her costume for the talent show.

9:23. "Want to see the fabric?" Rory asks.

9:24. *Please, Dorarian. Please.*

9:25. What will I do if she doesn't show?

9:26. "You wouldn't believe how amazing it is to get a dress made for you—Kirsten, are you even listening?"

"Oh, sorry," I say. Why did I ever think I could do this?

And then Dorarian's blue glasses peer through the window. She strides confidently into class. "Matteo, I need to talk to you, sir." Her voice is irritated like it always is when a book is way overdue. There isn't the slightest hint she doesn't mean it.

Matteo's face caves. Oops. I forgot to tell him this part. He hurries after Dorarian with his head down like a bad dog.

Brianna is standing by Matteo's backpack. But so is Hair Boy. Will she steal it with Hair Boy standing right there?

I wave my arm wildly in the air. "Mr. Balderis, I think I'm supposed to be working with Hair Boy," I say.

"Kirsten!" Rory whispers. "Hello? We're working together? Where have you been?"

141

Hair Boy looks at me like I'm nuts. "I'm not doing extra credit," he tells Balderis. "I don't even know what she's talking about."

Balderis checks his book. "I've got you down with Rory."

"Oh. Yeah, that's right," I mutter.

9:28. When Hair Boy goes back to his desk, I have to believe Brianna's done. I take a deep breath, walk up to Balderis's desk, leave my note, and sit down.

Balderis doesn't see. He's busy arguing with Sophie about how many points she has. "I have the second assignment as late." He taps his book. "And that's twenty points off."

9:29. "It was not late," Sophie says.

"Sophie, it was late. End of discussion," Balderis says.

Good, yeah. End of discussion. Read it. Read it. Read it. He's never going to see it.

9:30. The bell rings. Brianna heads for the door. *Balderis, come on. The note!*

"Brianna," Balderis calls as she breezes past.

"What?"

"I need to check your backpack."

"Why?"

"I believe I saw you taking something that wasn't yours. I'm probably wrong. Humor me."

"You can't check my backpack," Brianna says, her tan skin suddenly going pale. "That's not right."

"Yes," Balderis says, "I can."

142

He takes her backpack and unzips it. Nothing in the front pocket. Nothing in the middle part. Nothing in the back part.

I dig my pen point into my leg.

"Your sweater, please?" he asks.

"Are you going to make me strip?" Brianna spits at him. "Because that's, like, illegal."

"No . . . but I do want to see your sweater." He holds his hand out.

Her face gets red. She does nothing.

"*Your sweater*, Brianna," Balderis says.

Brianna slips off her sweater and hands it to Balderis. Balderis puts his hand in the pocket. He pulls out a battered green organizer. He opens it up: Two quarters and Matteo's library card fall out.

Kirsten

THIRTY-EIGHT

Walk

Back in English class, two elbows are on Walk's desk even before the bell rings.

"You think I don't know you set me up?" Brianna asks.

"What are you talking about?" Walk says.

"Matteo would never do this. It was you who told Kirsten what to do."

"Nobody set you up. You stole Matteo's test and you got caught," Walk whispers.

"Do you know how much I've been looking forward to the talent show? It is my whole life. You don't know. I have *nothing* without this," she says in one sobby breath; her eyes well up, tears roll down her cheeks.

"Oh, boo-hoo, boo-hoo, Brianna." Walk rolls his eyes.

She stops crying. Her eyes narrow. "I can make Matteo do whatever I want, you know."

"Oh, really? Well, if that's true, why'd you have to steal the test? Why didn't he just give it to you?"

She glares at Walk, grabs her pencil, and stalks off to the pencil sharpener.

When she comes back, she leans in real close. "I would be careful if I were you," she whispers.

"You do anything to Matteo's mom and I will—"

"What? What will you do?" She runs her hand along Walk's arm.

"Get off me." He shakes her hand away.

THIRTY-NINE

Kirsten

My mom has a headache again today. She must feel really lousy to let me make dinner again. Usually she does everything in her power to keep me away from the refrigerator. I check on her, but she's lying on her bed with the blinds pulled.

I find some frozen taquitos in the back of the freezer and zap them in the microwave. Kippy and I take them to the basement to eat. We spend all evening down there until I see her with her eyes closed and her cheek glued with drool to her *Life Cycle of Trees* book. I get her up to her room and she crashes on her bed.

My dad comes home just after that. I tell him Mom is sick again and he goes up to their room and closes the door. He doesn't come out, so I head for the garage to the Costco stash.

My mouth is spicy, salty, corny, happy as I munch on Barb-B-Q flavored Fritos. I cram a bag of Ruffles potato chips in my pocket for later. I wonder if Dr.

Markovitz could prescribe diet pills? I'm just imagining myself in a size three bikini when I hear voices. I dive behind my dad's new hybrid SUV, the crinkling and crumpling of the potato chip bag loud in my ears.

"Why is the light on out here?" my mom asks.

I don't move. Don't breathe.

"I didn't leave it on," my father says.

"You must have! You went back out to get your laptop in your car, remember?"

"That was last night."

"No," my mother barks.

"Yes it was."

"No it wasn't."

I guess it's good to know they talk directly to each other once in a while, even if it is just to fight. I put my hands on the cold cement floor to take some of the pressure off my knees. Inch by slow inch I slide forward and put my butt down. The chip bag makes a slight crinkling, crackling noise. My whole body freezes. *Can they see me?*

"You're making too much of this," my father says.

"How can you stand there and say that?"

I breathe out slowly, silently. They didn't hear. They think they're alone.

"Didn't you see them last week?"

"I saw them. They're friends. What is the big deal?"

"Rebecca says they're more than friends," my mom says. "Rebecca says Kirsten is more than friends with several boys."

147

"But you asked Kirsten and she said no. And I believe her. I've never liked Rebecca, you know that."

"Oh, you're so infuriating! Don't you even care about this?"

"Yes, I care. I just don't think it's worth getting all worked up about."

"You just like hurting me, don't you?" my mom asks.

"For Christ's sake, Rachel, it has nothing to do with you. How many times do I have to tell you that?"

"Didn't it ever occur to you that this might be awkward?"

"We've been over this a hundred times. I didn't think you'd find out."

"Why didn't you tell me? Why would you lie to me?"

"I never lied."

"Oh, don't even . . . You have a secret love child and you have the gall to tell me you didn't lie."

Wait a minute. "A secret love child"?

"I didn't lie. I just didn't mention it. He's my son. What do you want me to do? Just pretend he doesn't exist?"

"Why now, all of a sudden? Why didn't you send him to private school before?"

"I didn't realize how bad his school was. Look, I'm trying to do the right thing here. Don't I get any credit for that? Sylvia asked me to help with this."

"I bet she did."

"I owe her that much, Rachel."

"There are other private schools in Marin County. Why this one? Did you want this to come out?"

"You're the one who looked into every school in the entire county. You're the one who picked Mountain. You said it was far and away the best. Those were your exact words." He sighs. "Look. I didn't marry Sylvia, I married you. Please. I'm asking, I'm begging. Can we move on?"

"Your daughter and your son may or may not be having some kind of romantic . . ."

"So what is it you'd like me to do, Rachel?"

"I want you to tell me the truth. I don't want to worry my daughter is dating her black half brother. I don't want to be humiliated in front of my friends!"

My mom slams the door so hard the latch pops the door in and out again, leaving it wide open. I hear the swish of her robe and the angry flap of her slippers on the stepping stones.

My father watches her go. He leans on the workbench and rests his head in his hands. Then he follows my mother into the house, gently closing the door behind him.

I'm shaking so hard it's like I'm freezing, but I'm not cold. Is this why they've been fighting so viciously the last few months? Because my mother found out my father had a son? This can't be true. I must be dreaming. I must be.

Kirsten

FORTY

Walk

Monday morning, when Sylvia drops Walk at school, Kirsten jumps out at him like she's a big old jungle cat. "I—I—" Her eyes are shiny like she's on something. She grabs his arm.

"What?" Walk asks.

"You never say much about your dad. Does he live with you?"

"He's dead."

"Your dad? How do you know?" she asks.

Walk juts his chin out. "How do I *know*?"

Her cheeks get all red. "I mean, when did he die?"

"He was a pilot in the Air Force. He died before I was born."

"You never met him?"

"Nope."

She bites her lip. "Do you have a picture?"

"Why?" Walk asks.

"I'd just like to, you know, um, see it sometime? Does he look like you?"

They're in Balderis's class now. Walk stops. "I don't know."

She looks at the room like she doesn't know where she is.

"When's your birthday?"

"My birthday?" Walk glances around for Matteo, but he's not here yet. "Why? You gonna bake me a cake?"

"I have to know." She follows Walk to his seat.

"August eighth," Walk tells her.

"Mine is June second," Kirsten whispers, her eyes all lit up shiny again.

"Kirsten, I'm glad we're having this little bonding moment, but . . ." He motions with his head to her desk where she's supposed to be sitting now.

The second bell rings.

Balderis is still in the hall. He doesn't see her.

"Go, Kirsten," Walk hisses. She seems to wake up and scuttle on over to her desk.

What is that girl's problem today?

FORTY-ONE

Kirsten

In my sock drawer are photos of my dad when he was Walk's age. For the last three days I've been obsessively comparing them with a picture of Walk I Googled. My father has blond hair. Walk has black curly hair, or so it seems. He shaves his head so it's hard to totally know. My father has blue eyes. Walk has brown eyes. And of course Walk's skin is dark. But not that dark. If I take away the idea that my dad and Walk are different races, there is a strong resemblance. Their noses and jawlines are similar, as is something else about their faces.

But Walk and I are both twelve . . . we're only two months apart. How could my father have . . .

And then there's the fact that I now have a brother who is black. What does that mean? What have I thought about black people? Nothing, really. I haven't even known anyone who is black. The guy at the post office. Some kids in my preschool. Everybody in my neighborhood is white.

I guess I thought different. Poor? Did I think poor? Oprah isn't poor, but she's a celebrity.

I don't think I ever thought much about Walk being black, because I know him and he's just Walk. What does he think about being black? What does it feel like?

I wonder if this makes me part black, too? Maybe it does. Is this a weird thing to think?

What does it mean to have a different skin color? I don't even know.

Kirsten

FORTY-TWO

Walk

Matteo has never missed school before. He never missed tutoring last summer, either. Once he told Walk he didn't miss a single day all last year. Not one.

As soon as Walk gets home, he grabs the phone and settles into the sofa with his legs kicked over the arm. "Hey, where were you?" Walk asks when Matteo answers.

"My cousin had a baby. I had to watch her other kids while she was in the hospital."

"Everything okay?"

"Sure, it's a boy. A little *bebito*."

"No, I mean with your mom and . . . her job. When you weren't there, I was . . ."

"Oh. Yeah. So far."

"Did you tell her about what happened with Brianna and the test—"

"No."

"Would she tell you if—"

"If she gets accused of something she didn't do?" Matteo snorts. "Yeah, I'd know. She'd be crying so loud, you'd hear her all the way at your apartment. Hey, we get any new math homework?"

"Nope."

"Good. Okay, well, you know, thanks—"

"For what?" Walk switches the phone to the other ear.

"For bein' a butthead, what do you think?"

"You call me a butthead, you end up flat on all sides like a GameCube. A broken one. All cube, no game."

Matteo laughs. "I'd like to see that."

"Come to school tomorrow, I'll give you a little demo," Walk tells him.

"I'll be there, man," Matteo says. "I will."

Walk

FORTY-THREE

Kirsten

I tried to talk to my mom, but she was gone all day Sunday on a yoga retreat—didn't even say goodbye. And then as soon as she got back, she was out the door to Madison's mom's house to address auction invitations. Last night she was busy reloading the dishwasher because no one ever loads it the way she likes and filling out a big stack of application forms so Kippy can go to a gifted kids program on Saturdays.

Okay, maybe she wasn't that busy. Maybe I didn't really want to talk to her about this. But I have to talk to someone.

In the kitchen Kippy is standing on the step stool stirring a big mess. She's making the kind of concoction she usually creates with bubble bath and shampoo in the tub only now she's mixing tea bags, coffee grounds, and tuna fish.

"What are you doing?" I ask.

"Making compost."

"For what?"

"The tree."

"Oh yeah. The tree. Are Mom and Dad up yet?" I ask, though one look at the kitchen should tell me the answer to that question.

"They had a big fight last night."

"Again?"

"I slept in their room, but it didn't help."

"You sleep in their room so they won't fight?"

She nods.

"Ah, Kip." She looks so small in my old Scooby-Doo pajamas. I put my arm around her and give her a hug. Hey, shouldn't she be dressed? This is a school day.

"Mom's got to drive us to school . . . ," I say.

Kippy shrugs. She cracks an egg and adds the shell to the mess in her jar. "What's the matter with them?" She looks up at me and waits.

"Mom and Dad?"

She nods.

Mom sometimes lies to Kippy. She tells her robbers don't know our address, kids don't ever die, and moms don't have children they don't love. Kip always knows when Mom's feeding her a load of crap, though, and she comes and talks to me about it.

"Mom found out something Dad did a long time ago and she's really mad at him."

"What'd he do?"

I rest my elbows on the counter and watch Kippy. She's grown, I suddenly realize. Her face isn't as round

Kirsten

as it used to be. "You hear anything weird when they argued?"

"No. What'd he do?" she asks again.

"I don't know for sure, Kip."

She looks at me, then back at her jar. I can almost feel her thinking terrible things. When you tell Kip you don't know, she figures it's because the glaciers are melting and we won't live through the week, anyway.

"I don't," I repeat, jutting my chin out.

Her eyes continue to stare at me. She doesn't blink.

"Okay, okay . . . ," I say. "Remember that kid Walk who was here doing homework with me last week?"

She nods.

"He's our half brother. His dad is our dad, but he has a different mom." I laugh at this. I laugh so hard I can hardly stand up.

Kippy does not laugh. "Is this a true story?"

I get quiet now. "Yes."

She bites her lip and her eyes go straight up like she's trying to add a big column of numbers in her head. "So Dad's sperm went inside Walk's mom, but how did it get in there?" she whispers.

"God, Kippy, do you have to be so literal?"

"Well?" she asks, her little forehead still furrowed like she's trying to make sense of this.

"Ask Mom about that. Oh no! Don't ask Mom about it! Don't! Don't say a word to Mom about any of this! Mom's going to flip out. Look, I'll explain later, okay?"

"At least it isn't lymphoma," Kip says, pouring olive oil into her jar.

"Lymphoma?"

"The silent killer," she whispers. "That's what they said on Mom's radio program. Nobody has lymphoma, right?" Her forehead furrows again.

"Nobody has lymphoma," I tell her.

"Is Walk going to move in with us?"

"I don't think so."

"Is he going to come to Thanksgiving?"

"I don't know."

"Does he have any pets?"

"I don't know that, either. Kip . . . just promise you won't say anything to Mom, okay?"

"Okay." She shrugs. She's back to work now, cracking another egg into her jar.

"Kirsten?" she asks as I dig through the refrigerator looking for something better to eat than lemon yogurt. "You'll always be my sister. That's never going to change . . . is it?"

Kirsten

FORTY-FOUR

Walk

Walk's deep in his science homework when the phone rings. Gotta be Sylvia. Walk would bet money on it, if he had money, but like a fool he spent it all on Jamal's soap.

Walk grabs the phone. "I'm busy doin' drugs, Momma, what do you think?"

"What?" a little girl's voice asks.

"Who is this?"

"Kippy."

"Kippy?"

"I called to see if you have any pets?"

"Pets? Why do you want to know?"

"It's important," she says.

"I have a Venus flytrap," Walk tells her.

"Really?" She sounds all excited. "Can I see?"

"Sure, yeah. Kirsten on the line?"

"No," Kippy says.

"No? How'd you get my number?"

"I looked it up in the blue Mountain School book.

I have another question," Kippy says. "Do you like bunk beds?"

"I guess."

"Do you like the bottom bunk or the top bunk?"

"The top."

"Oh." She sighs. "Well, at least you like them. Kirsten likes them too. My mother won't let us get any, though."

"Glad we got that straightened out. Anything else you want to know? Do I sleep standing up? Do I wear shoes to bed?"

"I'm sorry," she whispers, "but this is new."

"What is new?"

"Having a brother. I never had one before."

"I'm *a* brother, Kippy, not *your* brother."

Kippy doesn't say anything, so Walk fills her in. "Black guys, we call each other brothers. Doesn't mean we really are related."

"African Americans?"

"Yeah, African Americans."

"Oh," she says. "Well, Kirsten said you are my half brother, so maybe the American is my half and the African is another girl's half. Do you have another sister?"

"Kirsten said *what?*"

"She said you are my half brother, but it's a secret and I shouldn't tell my mom."

"Kirsten is out of her mind."

"Is not."

"I'm not your half brother."

161

"Okay, okay," she says in a small voice. "But could I still see your Venus flytrap?"

Kip's a little kid. Little kids get their facts all mixed up. Kirsten said a brother . . . Kip thought she said *my* brother . . . It's a joke, right?

In Sylvia's bedroom Walk yanks on the file drawer. It's locked. Walk didn't know she kept it locked. The lock is tiny. Where would she keep a tiny key? Now he remembers there is a little key on the chain with the extra house key Sylvia has hidden under the palm tree pot.

At the front door he tilts the big palm forward. Big key, little key. Sylvia can't hide anything from him.

Walk pulls open the heavy broken, sagging drawer. Sylvia's writing is on the files. AUTO INSURANCE, AUTO LOANS, BIRTH CERTIFICATES. *Birth Certificates.*

There it is. WALKER WILBURT JONES with a tiny baby footprint on the back. The front says: MOTHER: SYLVIA ROODELMAN, FATHER: CLIMPTON JONES.

Of course it does. Stupid fool. What'd he think?

Walk pokes around to see what else is in here. A CLIMPTON file. Empty. He shoves the drawer closed and pulls out the bottom one. LEASE, MUTUAL FUNDS, NURSING BOOK LISTS, NURSING CLASSES, RECIPES, REPORT CARDS. Report cards: Walk flips through all of them. Almost all As. A couple of Bs and one C in third grade.

His last report card at City had all As and one A plus. He puts it back and takes it out again. He gets a little buzz looking at it. Gotta have one last peek. That's when he sees the pencil scratching on the inside back of the file: MWM, *Mount Tamalpais Hospital, 1350 South Sycamore Drive, Greenbrae, CA 94904.*

That must be where he was born. Only he wasn't born there. He was born at Oakland Children's, where Sylvia works.

MWM?

In the kitchen, Walk looks for the blue book with names and addresses of the kids at Mountain. His fingers sweat on the blue cover. M for McKenna. *Kirsten McKenna. Parents: Rachel and Mac W. McKenna.*

MWM.

Walk looks up Mount Tamalpais Hospital in the phone book, dials the number. Just hang up now, fool, he tells himself. "May I speak to Dr. Mac McKenna?"

"One moment and I'll connect you."

Walk kills the call with his thumb.

Sylvia used the folder as scratch paper. It doesn't mean anything. Walk erases so hard he burns white streaks in the manila. The name is gone. All gone.

Walk gets his swim gear and heads for the Y. He doesn't care that he already swam today. In the water he knows this is all one big fool mix-up. Every lap he knows it. . . . Thirty laps, thirty more, thirty after that.

The water is heavy, like wet sand. His shoulders are sore, his legs ache, but he keeps going, keeps on going until he sees Sylvia's white nurse shoes at the edge of the pool.

Walk

"What the heck you doing, scaring me half to death? You couldn't call and tell me where you're gonna be? Your hand fall off? Your mouth froze shut? You better hope it did, boy. You better pray it did." She's ranting, but he knows from her sound, she's more relieved than mad.

"What's the matter with you?" She tosses Walk a towel.

"Sorry," Walk mutters.

"Don't you sorry me." Sylvia shakes her finger at him.

They walk to the car, parked one wheel over the yellow curb. She grunts. "You look pale. You're coming down with something."

"No."

"You better say yes if you're hoping for dinner tonight or any other night the rest of your life."

"Yes," Walk says.

When they get home, she makes a sick-at-home meal, bagels and chicken soup. They're quiet at dinner. Just the TV noise and the spoons clack-clacking the bowls.

When the dishes are done, Sylvia cracks her big gray nursing manual to prepare her lecture. She glances up at Walk. "No homework tonight?"

Walk shrugs.

"Momma," he says.

"Um-huh."

164

"My middle name . . . where did it come from?"

Her body gets still like it's her funeral now. Only her eyes move. "It was just a name I thought of."

"*Wilburt* was a name you thought of?"

She grabs the remote control.

"Momma, do you send my report cards to MWM?"

Her head swivels so fast she doesn't need to answer.

"Why, Momma?"

Sylvia rests her head on her thumb. "What makes you think I do that?"

"Kippy told me, Momma. Know who Kippy is?"

Sylvia sucks her cheek in; her eyes go tiny in her head. She knows who Kippy is.

Walk

FORTY-FIVE

Kirsten

W hat do you mean you called him up?"

She shrugs a tiny shrug like she's going to get in trouble for just moving her shoulders. "I called him up. His number's in the book."

"Kippy!"

"You told me not to tell Mom. You didn't tell me not to tell Walk," she whispers.

"I didn't think you'd call him up."

"You didn't know if he had any pets, Kirsten. He's my brother," she whispers. "I have to know that."

"And you told him we were his sisters?"

She nods.

"Did it sound like he already knew that?"

Kippy shakes her head.

"Are you sure he understood? This is important, Kip. Try to remember exactly what he said."

She sticks her tongue out of her mouth and screws her face up. "He said all guys call each other brother. That doesn't mean they're really brothers."

"Ahhh. So he didn't believe you."

"He said you were crazy. He said if we get bunk beds he wants the top bunk."

"You asked him about bunk beds?"

She scrunches up her face like she knows she's going to tell me the wrong answer. "I was thinking maybe now Mom would let us get one. We could get a triple-decker."

Kirsten

FORTY-SIX

Walk

When he opens the door, there's Aunt Shandra on the stoop looking way orangey, like she was tagged orange all over.

"What are you doing here?" Walk asks.

"What are *you* doing here?" Shan answers.

This is Walk's second day home from school and he doesn't plan to go back.

"Okay, so I wanted to have a little talk. What's your excuse?" Shan asks.

Walk shrugs.

"Jamal doesn't give me enough trouble, you start acting up on me." She puts her hands on her hips. "C'mon, let's go."

"I'm not dressed."

"Don't need a tux where we're going."

"These are my pajamas."

She stares at his shorts and T-shirt. "How's a person supposed to know that? Go on then, get yourself dressed."

Walk throws some clothes on, heads outside.

Shan unlocks the car door. "Ice cream? Candy? CDs? Johnny Walker? What you think we need first here, guy?"

"You can buy me a BMW all tricked out, it's not gonna help, Shan."

"Well, that's what's wrong with you, nephew. A BMW would be mighty fine. I'd do a lot for a BMW."

She waits for Walk's answer. When he doesn't say anything, she turns the ignition on. "Run over to Burger King, I guess," she mutters. "Sylvia is right about one thing. You one mad dog . . ."

Burger King is practically in Walk's backyard, it's that close. But Shan would drive from her bedroom to her living room if she could.

"Look Walk, I want you to hear this from me."

"Little late for that."

"Now you listen to me." She points her long nail at Walk. "Your momma loved Climpton. Sun rose when he came in, set when he left. He was that handsome. And charm, that man had it big time."

"He isn't my father. I don't care."

Shan stamps her foot on the brake and stares at Walk. "Let's get this straight. I'm doin' the talking, you're doin' the listening."

Walk hunkers down in his seat.

"Sylvia fell hard for Climpton, but Climpton wasn't ready to get tied down. He didn't want any part of nothing permanent. And then one day at work

Walk

she met Mac. Mac was working at Oakland Children's then, too."

Walk cracks the door. "We gettin' out or what?"

She drums her nails on the dashboard. "Yeah, all right," she says, opening up. "What are you gonna have?"

"Two cheeseburgers, fries, and a Coke." He might as well get a free meal out of this.

At the table, Sylvia pokes her straw into her cup cover, making shrieky little noises like plastic people are dying in there. She unwraps her burger and starts up again. "And then Sylvia gets pregnant, which she was real happy about."

"Was she still with McKenna when she found out?"

"Nope."

"She's alone, she's pregnant. Oh, I bet she's happy." Walk jams three fries down his throat.

"I said *she was happy*," she snaps at Walk. "Course, I thought she was out of her fool mind. But she wanted a family and if she couldn't have Climpton and a baby, she wanted the baby. So don't you tell me you weren't wanted because that's a load of crud. You hear me? That woman would give her life for you and you know it."

Walk stuffs his cheeseburger practically whole in his mouth and chokes it down.

"One day she's big as a house, and she stops in at one of them baby stores and there was Mac with

Rachel, who had a belly on her, too. You know who that was?"

"Kirsten," Walk snorts.

"Ya-huh. Well, Mac, he called Sylvia and Sylvia told him, 'Um-huh, it's yours.' So he started sending money. She didn't ask for it, he just sent it. I liked him better after that."

"How's she know my dad's McKenna?"

"How's she know?" Shan's voice screeches so high the people in the next booth stop talking. "Look, mister, I am sorry you don't like this. But you say something like that again, I'm going to make it so you never sit down the rest of your life. You getting married, you standin' up, you die standin' up, too, you understand me, boy?"

Walk grinds a french fry into the ketchup.

"McKenna checked in every few months. He's proud about you, about how smart you are, wants to know this and that. When Sylvia decides to pull you out of public school, he says he'll pay for Mountain."

"I got a *scholarship* to Mountain," Walk tells her

She makes a funny blowing noise with her orange-lipstick lips. "Scholarship covered fifteen hundred dollars. So, McKenna, he only had to pay eighteen big ones. Pediatric ICU nurses don't have eighteen thousand dollars sittin' around, Walk."

Walk puts his hands over his ears. She waits until he brings them down again.

"Look." She takes hold of Walk's chin between

171

her fingers, her nails clicking against themselves. "Who your parents are don't make a difference. Nobody has any choice in the matter. You aren't any different than anyone else in that. You are what you make of yourself and don't you ever forget it."

"Yeah, sure, but now I'm half white."

"What you talking about, boy?" She grabs his arm. "That ain't half white. That's black as the night is long. This doesn't mean anything except you got your school paid for. Do you hear me?" She squeezes tighter.

"I got a white dad and all it means is I got my school paid for? You're wrong about that." He pulls his arm back. "So, so, so wrong."

FORTY-SEVEN

Kirsten

Matteo has this tiny chess set in his notebook. At lunch he teaches me how to play. This is kind of okay-fun, but the table is lonely without Walk. Even Jade and Hair Boy are subdued without him.

On the way to the library we run into Rory.

"I need to talk to you, Kirsten," she snaps.

Oh great.

Matteo zips and unzips his binder. He rolls his lips in and pulls his eyelids down low over his eyes. Matteo's expressions are pretty subtle, but I'm beginning to be able to read them. He hates Rory. That much is clear.

"What?" I ask when Matteo leaves.

"It's only because you can't sing." Rory spits the words at me.

"What's only because I can't sing?"

"You had to mess it up, didn't you?"

"Had to mess what up?"

"The talent show. Brianna told me you and your new boyfriends or whatever they are set her up so she'd get caught stealing Matteo's organizer. And now she's mad at *me* about it."

"I don't know what you're talking about."

"Yes you do. I know when you're lying. You do that flutter thing with your hand. You forget I've known you for five years. I know *everything* about you."

"Brianna was forcing Matteo to do her homework and give her test answers. If he wouldn't do what she said, she'd tell her mom that Matteo's mom was breaking things."

"Matteo's mom's her maid. You're going to worry about somebody's *maid?*"

"What's that supposed to mean?"

"Just what I said. Besides, Brianna wouldn't do that. That's just crazy."

"You know she would. You used to know that, anyway. I don't know what you know now."

"It was you and that black guy who did this. Does your mom even know about *him?*"

I can't help snickering at this. If Rory only knew.

"Why are you laughing? What's the matter with you?"

I shrug.

"She doesn't know, does she?"

"Yes she does," I tell her.

"You never used to be petty like that just because you couldn't be in the talent show. Spoil it for everyone. You know they canceled the whole thing, don't you?"

"Why?"

"Like I know why they're canceling. Probably because Brianna can't be in it so her mom isn't paying."

"They did it last year without all that extra money."

"Yeah, but Brianna was in it last year. If Jacqueline Hanna-Hines doesn't want it to happen, I guess it doesn't happen," she whispers. "And Brianna is blaming me because I'm the one who told her about Matteo's test. Me? I am *so* innocent here."

"Choose better friends, Rory. I mean, *Brianna*? You call *her* your friend?"

"Hello? She's, like, really popular. You could be popular, too. But you don't even try. You just want to feel sorry for yourself."

"I don't feel sorry for myself."

"My mom says I'm supposed to be nice because your parents are getting a divorce, but I'm so sick—"

"Shut up!" I cover my ears with my hands. "Just shut up!"

I'm not sure how I get to the library, but that's where I find myself, with my head facedown on the table. And then the next thing I know, Matteo is tapping my shoulder. "You okay?" he asks. "You look like you're going to pass out or something."

A few minutes later he scoots a Dixie cup full of water in my direction. "Here. Dorarian says to drink this."

Kirsten

FORTY-EIGHT

Walk

No way Walk's sitting locked in the car with Sylvia clear to church and back.

Walk was hoping she'd stay at Aunt Tanesha's all afternoon, all week . . . forever'd be good. But Sylvia's back again, in his face, digging in his closet, pulling out his old suit.

"Too small," he mumbles.

She makes a face. "Try it on."

"Why? Somebody die?"

"Just put it on."

Walk jams his arm in. Shoulders so tight he's a humpback. Guess it's been a while since he's been to a funeral.

She clucks like she does when the phone bill's too high. "Wear what you wear to church," she decides.

"Where we going?"

"We're meeting mkmakana," she says like her mouth is full of biscuits.

"What?"

"We're meeting Mac McKenna," she repeats.

Walk wads up the jacket and tosses it at her. "You outta your mind?" He brushes by Sylvia, pockets her keys on the way out the door. This isn't his plan, he just sees them there and suddenly he has them in his hand. Sylvia's still standing in his room. She can't see what he's doing out here.

He slams the front door—he knows that bugs her—and goes straight for her car. He heads for the driver's seat, jams the keys in the ignition. The motor turns over then catches.

Walk slips the transmission to *R* and steps on the gas pedal. The car shoots backward. His head yanks back. His toe finds the brake, pushes down, and the car jerks to a stop. Sweat drops off his face. He forgot to check what was back there. Luckily, nothing.

He moves the transmission to *D* and hits the gas again. The car jumps forward. He pushes down harder. It goes faster. Harder. Faster. His apartment disappears. His neighbors. The apartments all down the street.

In the car he sees Sylvia's cell hanging from the cigarette lighter. Out the window is the mailbox he once crashed into on his bike. The neighbor kid in her Girl Scout uniform.

But how fast can the car really go? He gives the car some gas. It leaps out of his hands, swerves right, then left. He slams the brakes, wipes the sweat off his hands.

Go slower for a while, he decides. Get the feel of it. His heart is cranking. Carefully, he pulls the car onto

177

Walk

the busy street. He lurches forward, faster, faster, then he sees the stoplight. The intersection. He hits the brakes. Waits for the green.

When the light changes, he pushes forward and turns off the main road. No problem. He even remembers to use the turn signal. They should let kids drive. It really isn't that hard.

Then suddenly a stop sign. A stop sign? Too late to stop now, but a pickup truck on his left thunders toward him. His foot slips on the brake. His arms stiffen for the crash. His hand flies up to protect his head. The brake. His foot is on the brake. He's stopped.

His heart beats so loud it's like it's somewhere on the dashboard. A car behind him honks.

It suddenly dawns on him he's in the middle of the road. He's shaking so hard he can hardly get the car out of there. He pulls over, his head crammed full of pictures of Sylvia at a funeral. His funeral.

He's still breathing hard, but he's okay. Everything is okay. He didn't even get a scratch on her precious car. He grabs Sylvia's cell and dials Matteo.

"You'll never guess what I'm doin'." He tries to sound cool now.

"Your math homework."

"I'm driving, man."

"Where?"

"No, *I'm* driving."

"What? The little rides in front of Toys 'R' Us?"

"No. Sylvia's car."

"Where's Sylvia?"

"At home."

"*Driving* driving?" Matteo asks.

"Uh-huh. I thought I might drive over to get you."

"Wait, who else is in the car?"

"Just me."

"On the freeway?"

Walk imagines himself gunning down the freeway. "Why not?"

"Why not?" Matteo gulps. "What's the matter with you, man?"

"No, really. I could come pick you up. No one'll know."

"Walk?" Matteo whispers. "What are you doing?"

Walk tries to answer, but his throat clogs all up. He hangs up so Matteo won't hear. What *is* he doing?

He dials Jamal.

"Walk? That you?"

"Yeah. I'm just gonna drive on over there."

"You and Sylvia?"

"No, just me. I got Sylvia's car."

"You *drivin'* Sylvia's car?"

"Mebbe."

Jamal laughs his fool head off. "You be in so much trouble, boy. She going to iron your sorry butt till it so flat you can't sit anymore."

"She's not going to find out."

"Yeah, right. You gonna drive Sylvia's cherry-new 350 on over here and no one's gonna know."

179

"That's right," Walk tells him, when he hears knocking on the window. The police. Stupid fool. What has he been thinking?

But it's not the police. It's Sylvia still in her blue churchgoing dress. She's so mad, she's shaking all over and spit is flying wild out of her mouth.

Sylvia points to the door lock. Walk clicks her cell off, flips the door button, and she slips in on the passenger side.

"What do you think you're doing?"

"Nothin'."

"Nothing? You ever pull a stunt like this again, I'll make you wish you weren't alive. Do you understand me?"

Walk looks at the wheel. Shines it with his thumb. Keeps shining but it gets duller the more he rubs. "It was you who lied, Sylvia, not me."

"We're talking about you driving my car."

"Does Jamal know?"

"Does Jamal know what?"

"You know what."

She waits like she doesn't want to go there. "No," she finally says.

"How about everyone else?"

She shakes her head. "Only Shan."

"Yeah, and she has a big mouth."

Sylvia's eyes waver. "Shan swore she hasn't told anyone. I don't think Jamal knows."

180

Walk snorts. "'Climpton this, Climpton that' my whole life. Is Climpton even dead?"

She breathes big and hard. "Yes," she finally says. "He died two years after you were born."

"I ever meet him?" Walk's voice cracks when he says this.

She shakes her head no.

"You even my mother? Or is that a big fat lie, too?"

She makes a noise then like her head is exploding off her body. Her hand shakes like it wants to slap him.

"You think I'd put up with this crap if you weren't my son?"

"I'm goin' back to City," Walk tells her. "I like it better."

Her eyes are so hot they're scorching his hair right off his head.

"You want to go back to City, be my guest. Just wait until the end of the semester, then you can go."

"You sure?"

"Yes I'm sure. And for what you've done today, you are grounded for your life, boy. Until you're eighty, do you hear me? You better hope, you better pray you never do this again."

Walk

FORTY-NINE

Kirsten

I'm down in the basement watching TV when I hear the slamming. *Vip. Vup. Bang.* Everything slammable is being slammed.

Kippy hops down the stairs. "Mom's mad."

"How come?"

Kippy shrugs. Her shoulders stay glued near her ears like she's forgotten them up there.

"Kirsten," my mom calls down, "I need to talk to you, *right now.* Kippy, Daddy saved a program on walruses. Would you like to watch it?"

"No, thank you," Kippy says.

My mother comes down. Her face looks like it has been scrubbed raw by a loofah. Everything is pink and puffy.

I know what she's going to say. She's going to tell me they're getting divorced, just like Rory said.

"You gotta try this one, Kippy. Walruses are amazing," Mom says.

Kip can't stand TV, which makes my mom proud, except for when she needs a babysitter.

Kippy's shoulders slump. "Do I have to?"

My mother nods her head.

I follow my mom to the dining room.

My mom sits down on one of the white chairs and leans in toward me. "You'd tell me if anything unusual happened, wouldn't you?"

I look at the hutch full of our good china. It stays in there. We never use it. The wall is painted to look like marble. There's a photo of our family dressed in jeans and white shirts in front of a waterfall at Yosemite. Everything looks perfect . . . too perfect.

"Kirsten?" My mom peers at me.

"What?"

"Anything . . . upsetting . . . ?" She reaches in her pocket and takes out a square of Ghirardelli chocolate and puts it in front of me.

"Mom? What's the matter with you?" I unwrap the square before she can change her mind.

"There's nothing wrong with a treat once in a while," my mother says.

My mouth fills with a full chocolate rush. "I know about Walk, if that's what you're asking," My eyes are focused on the table. The earnest tone of the walrus video comes up from the basement. "I know who Walk is . . ."

"I told him she would tell. *I told him*," she says.

Kirsten

"Told who? Who would tell?"

She dives for the phone and starts dialing.

"No, wait. Mom, who?"

"Sylvia. Walk's mother. Your father said she wouldn't tell, but I knew she would."

"Walk's mother didn't tell me."

"Of course not. Walk told you."

"No. I found out from *you*."

She cuts the call off and looks at me.

"*Me?*"

"You and Daddy in the garage last week. It was late, eleven or twelve, I think. You didn't know I was there."

"What were you doing sneaking around the garage at eleven at night?"

I twist my ring around and around.

"Kippy's chips," she whispers. "You ate all those chips, Kirsten?"

I don't answer.

"All of them?" she repeats in a pinched voice.

"No, not all of them," I spit back.

"How many?"

"Mom, do you have to *count* everything?"

She sighs. "Kirsten, what am I going to do with you?"

"Nothing. It's not your problem, it's my problem."

"Yes, and I'm trying to help you with your problem."

"Yeah, but your help doesn't help."

Anger blazes in her eyes. She takes a deep breath and seems to try to control it. "Okay. What are *you* going to do about *your* problem?"

"I'm going back to Dr. MarkoWitzo Ritz Bits or whatever her name is," I tell her, though this surprises even me. I hadn't given this a moment's thought until now, but I'm suddenly glad I've said it.

"Oh." Her voice wavers, like she's tripped on one of Kippy's shoes. "Good," she adds shakily. "I'm . . . That's very good." She smiles a small, real smile.

"What I started to say was I'm sorry about the food, but I'm not sorry about Walk. I wasn't sure about it at first. But you know what? I really like Walk. I really do."

"Kirsten, this isn't all about you." She stands up and heads for the front stairs.

"Actually, it is about me," I tell the back of her crocheted top. "Walk's my brother."

She freezes with her foot on the first step. "Your brother and your dad's son and what about me?" She takes a sobby breath. "You're two months apart, Kirsten. I can just hear Rebecca and Linda and Jacqueline. Oh, Jacqueline." She sinks down and sits in a heap on the step. "'Oh my god, Rachel'"—my mother does a high-pitched imitation of Jackie Hanna-Hines— "'your Mac was a busy boy.'"

"Doesn't sound like she's much of a friend."

"There are friends and there are friends," my mother says. "The way to handle this is with style. Set the tone like this is a United-Colors-of-Benetton kind of thing: 'Everyone should have a stepson who is African American.'"

I frown at her. "Mom? Is that what the problem is?"

My mom doesn't answer.

"It's about who Walk is inside, Mom. Not what color—"

"I know that. Of course I know that."

"Do you?"

She sighs, tips her head forward, and massages the bridge of her nose with her thumb. "This is too hard, Kirsten. I want this to be someone else's problem."

I reach over and take her hand. She squeezes my fingers so I know she's glad I'm doing it. We sit like this for a few minutes.

"Mom, I have a question. Did Dad cheat on you?"

She shakes her head. "No. We had a stormy relationship. On again, off again. And when it was on again, it was on again. And when it was off again, we were never going to see each other ever again. One of those off-again times . . ."

"Dad started going out with Sylvia?"

"Uh-huh."

"Why'd you get married?"

"Why'd we get married?" She sighs. "We had you. You were such a wonderful baby. What a love you were . . . and you still are." She squeezes my hand again. "We wanted to give you a proper family. And I love your dad. I always have. If I didn't, this would all

186

be so much easier. But this. I wasn't expecting this. Can you imagine keeping a secret like this for thirteen years? What kind of a person does that?"

"Are you . . ." I clear my throat, scratch at the table with my nail.

"Kirsten," my mom snaps. "Do you have any idea how much that table costs?"

"Getting divorced?" I ask.

She doesn't answer.

"You are, aren't you?" I whisper.

"No."

"No?"

"I don't think so." Her mouth twitches. "I'm not sure."

"But it isn't for sure yes."

"No, it's not for sure yes."

I breathe out a huge gasp of air and close my eyes.

Kirsten

FIFTY

Walk

Walk picks up the phone. It's Matteo. "Hey, you have the flu or something?"

"Ringworm."

"Very funny. You really sick?"

"What, you're my mother?"

"Fine, man, I won't call you."

"Hey, I'm sorry, okay?"

"You want the math homework?" Matteo asks.

Who cares about the math homework? Not Walk. He doesn't care about anything. "Yes," he says.

"It's pages one thirty-five and six. Supposed to do all the problems. Be careful of number eight. If it's really easy, you're doing it wrong," Matteo says.

"How's it tricky? Wait, I'll get my book." Walk has the book in his hand when the doorbell rings. He holds the phone with his shoulder. "Okay, page one thirty-five," he says as he opens the door.

Walk's stomach sinks low. Mac McKenna is standing there with a guitar case in his hand. Something roars like a train through Walk's head.

"Number eight. Got it? Walk? You there?" Matteo jammers in his ear.

"I ga-gotta go," Walk mutters to Matteo.

"Whoever said doctors don't make house calls?" McKenna says.

Walk doesn't look him in the eye. "I'm not sick."

"I know." McKenna sets the guitar down, sticks his hand in his pocket. His face twitches into a sorry smile. "May I come in?"

Walk doesn't move, doesn't even breathe.

"Give me two minutes." McKenna holds up two fingers.

The door swings shut in Mac McKenna's face. Walk just let it go. He didn't really slam it. Sylvia would kill him for slamming the door in somebody's face. Somebody's white face.

"I understand how you must be feeling," McKenna calls through the closed door.

Walk stands so still he can feel the blood moving inside him. His blood.

It seems to take forever before Mac McKenna's footsteps walk back down the path. The ignition catches; the car moves away.

Walk goes into Sylvia's room, finds his birth certificate, and blacks out his middle name. It isn't his

Walk

name anymore. He's not Walker Wilburt Jones. He's Walker Jones now.

But Jones is Climpton's name.

Walk's name is . . . Roodelman?

Roodelman is a joke.

What is his name?

He doesn't even know.

FIFTY-ONE

Kirsten

I know Sylvia looks at Walk's email. But he's not
answering his phone, so what am I supposed to do?

> *Walk,*
> *This is way weird. Look, I need to talk 2 u.*
> *Kirsten*

Send

> *P.S. It's important.*

Send

> *Answer your phone.*

Send.

> *C'mon!*

Send.

When I get to Balderis's class the next day, there's

something on my desk. It's a piece of blue-lined note-book paper all folded up like a package. KIRSTEN, it says in Rory's loopy writing.

Matteo comes over to my desk. "Rory put it there," he whispers. We both look down at the home-made envelope like it's a bomb.

I unfold the paper. Inside is a page torn out of a magazine. A Weight Watchers ad. I hear Rory laughing across the room.

Matteo sees the page. He takes a quick look down like he has never noticed my body before. Then he crushes the ad and tosses it in the garbage.

He comes back, sits down, and starts working. We both pretend we are busy with other things, but I can see him steal little glances at me.

"What?" I ask.

His face goes from brown to sunburned brown. Even his ears seem suddenly to be tinted red. "You don't need that," he whispers. "You look . . . good."

Now my face feels flushed, too. He's not Rory. This isn't a lie. This is what he really thinks.

It's the nicest thing a boy has ever said to me.

I'm still thinking about what Matteo said when Walk shows up. He avoids my eyes. His face shuts me out.

He knows.

All through class Walk keeps tight to himself, and when the bell rings he disappears. I don't see him in the hall. I don't see him at lunch. Finally after school I track him down at his locker. One glance at me and he spins the dial and moves away.

"Hey! Wait! What did I do?" I run after him.

"What did you do?" he spits the words at me.

"Yeah," I say breathing hard. "What did I do?"

"You knew all along," he says.

"No I didn't."

He snorts.

"No really! I only found out last week."

"You're lying."

"No. NO!"

"You found out and then you told the whole world."

"I didn't tell the whole world. Just Kippy. Nobody else."

"I don't believe you."

"Fine, but it was just Kippy."

His eyes look quick at me under their dark lashes.

"Yeah . . . but who'd she tell?"

"Just you."

He scowls like he doesn't believe this. Then shrugs. "It doesn't matter. January I'm out of here."

"You're leaving Mountain."

"*Yeah.*"

We walk side by side, then he suddenly speeds up. I chase after him. "Why?"

He doesn't answer. His legs keep moving, long and fast. "How'd you find out?" he asks, suddenly stopping.

"I overheard my parents fighting about it. My

Kirsten

mom found out from some financial planner person last spring. The guy messed up and put a bank account number she didn't know about on his report. She started snooping and found out my dad was paying your school bill out of it."

"I got a *scholarship!*" he shouts.

"Okay, okay." I raise my hands.

His eyes move quick from side to side.

I start in again. "I knew my parents weren't married when they had me. My mom told me that a long time ago. I swear that's all I knew."

He nods, his head barely moving.

"This is weird," I say. "But it's not my fault."

He doesn't answer.

I put my hand on his arm. "Look, you don't have to leave. Couldn't we just pretend this never happened?"

He shakes my arm off like I'm something nasty spilled on him. "No," he whispers. "We can't."

FIFTY-TWO

Walk

When Walk gets home he calls Jamal.

"Hey, I'm coming back, man," Walk says.

"To City?"

"Ya-huh."

"No kiddin'? Sylvia's letting you?"

"Yep."

"Why?" Jamal asks.

"Why?"

"City's a sewer," Jamal says. "How much they give you, anyway?"

"Who?" Walk asks.

"Mountain."

"Scholarship money? A lot, man. A whole lot," Walk says.

Jamal is quiet so long, Walk thinks his cell has gone dead. "You still there?"

"Yeah, I'm still here. I only got fifteen hundred dollars," Jamal says.

"Whaddya you talkin' about? From Mountain? You applied?"

"You think you the only one got plans, man?"

"You got in?"

"What you take me for, Walk, some kind of fool? Course I got in. Just couldn't get the moneys together is all. I been trying. I made nine hundred bucks."

"Selling soap?"

"Amway," Jamal barks. "Pretty good, huh?"

Walk says nothing.

"Walk, you there?"

"Yeah," Walk whispers. "It's good, Jamal. It's really good."

FIFTY-THREE

Kirsten

My father is sitting behind his desk staring at his computer screen. I think he's working, but his hands don't touch the keyboard. I peek behind him. The screen is off. He's staring at a blank screen? "Dad?"

No answer. Dr. Dad is silent as a tree.

I look around his office. On the wall, he has his diplomas from Cal and Stanford, a picture of him with some people in tie-dyed shirts, photos of me and Kippy.

I point to the pictures. "You going to put Walk up there?"

"How do you suppose your mother would feel about that?" he mutters.

"She'll get used to it. You know how Mom is. She hates to be left out. Why didn't you tell her? Why didn't you tell me?"

"I knew your mom would flip out. Sylvia wanted

to do it all herself. What was I supposed to do?" he snaps.

"He's my brother. Didn't you think I needed to know that?"

He nods and goes silent again. "Your brother . . . my son." He puts his head in his hands. I figure this is going to be the end of the conversation, when suddenly he blurts out, "You know the last few years I've been going down to the Y to watch Walk swim."

I don't know what to make of this: my father pretending to be a stranger watching a kid who doesn't know he's his son.

"I had this idea that if he went to Mountain with you, I could have all my kids together. Maybe I wanted you to find out. Maybe I did."

"I'm glad I know. That's for sure. Walk's great, Dad. Really. Everybody likes him. *He's* brilliant."

My father raises his head and smiles.

"Kippy's brilliant, too. All your kids are brilliant except one."

My father looks up at me. "You're brilliant, too."

"No I'm not. I'm not stupid. I don't mean that. But I'm just, you know, *normal.* I'm not a math whiz. I don't even like science."

"You have to work for things. Give yourself a chance. You can't expect everything to be easy. But yes, I know you aren't a math whiz and you don't like science."

"Why do you always say I'm brilliant, then? It's like you're making fun of me."

"I'm not making fun of you," he says softly. "I do think you're brilliant."

"No you don't."

"Yes I do. Some people's brilliance is in their head. A surgeon's brilliance is in her hands. But there are people who have brilliant hearts. They shine right through them."

"Oh yeah, that's worth a lot," I mutter.

"It is worth a lot. It's worth everything . . . You know when I knew you were really special? You were about four and I took you down to the Berkeley free clinic with me. One of the nurses gave you a little bag of Halloween candy, then the next thing I knew you'd disappeared. Couldn't find you anywhere. Thought I was going to have a heart attack. Finally found you in the park across the street handing out your candy to the homeless people. You didn't need that candy and they did. Even at four you knew this."

"You cried when you found me. I didn't get it. I wasn't lost."

"Yeah." He nods, smiling at this. "I know."

I've heard this story before, but not for a long time. It feels good to remember the little person I was. Is that who I still am?

"I need you, Daddy. You're never around anymore."

"I'm an internist. It's not a nine-to-five job."

199

Kirsten

"You've always been an internist. You didn't used to be gone all the time."

He picks up the stapler on his desk and inspects the bottom, checks it for staples, and closes it again. "I don't like to fight with your mom," he mutters.

"So don't fight with her."

"It's not that easy."

"You can't expect everything to be easy," I mimic him.

He smiles at this. "You're not supposed to pay attention to *everything* I say." He gives me a playful cuff on the side of the head.

"So what are we going to do now?" I ask.

"You're going to figure out how to include Walk in our family."

"*I* am? Me? But what about you?"

"You don't think I've made a mess of the whole business? I see more in you than you see in yourself, Kirsten. Just the way you are with Kippy . . . Do you know how special that is?"

"But Dad . . ."

"If you could make that kind of connection with Walk, you'd move the earth an inch or two in the right direction. I'm depending on this part of you," he whispers, touching his heart, "right here."

"Yeah, but . . ." My voice trails off.

His eyes are so clear, so true. He really believes I can do this. He really does.

FIFTY-FOUR

Walk

So how was school today?" Sylvia asks when Walk comes in.

"Fine." Walk goes to his room and shuts the door.

Sylvia knocks. "I was thinking of making pork chops for dinner. Sound good?"

"Um-huh."

The handle turns. She stands in Walk's doorway. "Been too long like this. We have to talk."

"Nothin' to talk about." Walk shrugs her off.

She doesn't budge.

"Someday you'll have your own kids. You'll make mistakes and you'll hope your kids forgive you."

Walk keeps his head down. His handwriting gets smaller and smaller.

"I hate City," she says. "I wanted you to have the chance to go to a better school."

"Done now?" Walk asks, without looking up.

"I'm glad you know."

"No thanks to you . . . Found out from some little kid I hardly know."

She sits down on Walk's bed. "We'll get through this, Walk." She puts her hand on his arm. He flicks it off.

She goes out, comes back a few minutes later with a blue envelope. She wiggles a letter out of the envelope one side then the other. The way she does this, Walk sees her hands have taken the letter out this carefully a hundred times before. She hands it to Walk.

October 21, 1994
Dear Sylvia,

I got a big fat grin on my face there's no wiping off. I love the pictures you sent of your baby son, Walker. I can tell by the light in his eyes, he's got your spunk, your sparkle, your intelligence. He's all you, Sylvia, right up to his little old man eyebrows. And I'm pleased as anything he has my name. It's a fine name and that's a fact. Tell him to use it with my blessings. I'll give him an earful myself when I get to meet him, which I'm hoping will be early next year.

I'm sorry things didn't work out between us, Sylvia. God knows I tried, but some things aren't meant to be. You're a wonderful woman and you'll make some lucky man one hell of a wife. May God bless you and your son with all the sweetness in his kingdom.

202

Then there's something been blacked all out. And then it says:

Climpton Jones

"What's this here?" Walk asks, his thumb on the scribbled-out square.

"Crossed it out."

"What'd it say?"

Sylvia sighs. "Don't know if I remember."

Walk looks at her. "Don't *know* if you remember? You either remember or you don't."

She sighs, chews down hard on her gum. "I was head over heels in love with the man, would lay down my life for him, and he signed it *'your friend'*?"

"So you crossed it out?"

"I gave you Climpton's last name because I wanted you to have a little of him. I named you Wilburt because Mac said it was a lucky name been in his family for a hundred years. If I'd been lucky, Climpton would have loved me the way I loved him."

"Climpton didn't care you took his name, even if you didn't get married?"

Sylvia's mouth bunches up. She stares up at the ceiling. "He didn't know I took his name," she admits. "A girl has to have her pride, you know. Look, I loved Climpton, but he didn't love me. Mac loved me, but I didn't love him. The world doesn't make sense sometimes."

"The world is a big mess," Walk says.

Walk

Sylvia puts her hand on Walk's cheek. She holds it there for the longest time. "How can I not love the world that gave me you?"

"How am I going to tell everyone about this, Momma?"

"Everyone who?"

"Jamal, Matteo, the kids at school."

"The kids at City?"

Walk shakes his head. "Mountain. I'm gonna stay," he mumbles.

"You what?"

"I'm gonna stay," he repeats.

"Why?"

"I like it better, that's why," Walk spits at her.

"Nothing wrong with that," she says softly.

"Everything's wrong with that," Walk says. "D'you know Jamal applied to Mountain? He got in, too. But he couldn't go because he didn't get enough scholarship money."

She raises her eyebrows. "That's why he's been selling everything isn't nailed down?"

"Yep."

"Well, I'll be."

"Matteo got a full scholarship. Jamal and I both got partial scholarships. But I get to go. Jamal doesn't."

"You don't think Tanesha would pay for Jamal if she could?"

"Of course she would. That's not the point."

"You're darn right she would. And so would I. And so did Mac. He wanted the best for you, same as I do. Same as Tanesha does for Jamal."

"But what about Jamal?"

"That boy is going to own the whole world one of these days. And god help him, he'll do it all his own way."

"And I'm supposed to tell him my white father is paying for me."

"Yes."

"That's all, just yes?"

"That's all, just yes."

Walk

FIFTY-FIVE

Kirsten

Don't sit here," Walk says.

"Why?" I ask.

But Jade and Hair Boy show up before he can answer. Jade has dyed the ends of her hair blue. "Got any candy?" She squints at me.

I shake my head.

"I do," Jade says. This is the first time Jade has ever shared her candy. She gives each of us a Jelly Belly, carefully considering which bean should go to which person. I get peach. Matteo gets mango and Walk gets Dr Pepper.

"What's up?" she asks Walk, who hasn't even looked to see which flavor he got.

Walk doesn't answer.

Jade squints one eye totally closed, puts her fingers in her mouth, and whistles so loud kids three tables down shut up.

Everyone stares at her. "You guys have been so creepy lately," she announces, grabbing my lunch and setting it in its usual spot next to Walk. She raps Walk on the head. "Get over yourself," she commands.

"What?" Walk asks.

Matteo drops his lunch on the table. "Matteo and I have been talking," Jade says. "We don't like this, do we, Matteo?"

Matteo looks at Walk. "We're all friends. You and Kirsten . . . Just, you know, figure it out, okay?"

"Yeah, like, talk or something," Jade says. She gets a grip on Hair Boy, who is carefully lining his sandwich with potato chips. "C'mon." She sticks his loose chips back in his lunch bag. Matteo picks up his lunch, too.

Walk grabs Kirsten's plastic spoon and raps it on the table. "Hey, wait! C'mon, don't leave. We're fine, aren't we, Kirsten? The best of friends. Look, I have her spoon."

Matteo and Jade don't turn around. Hair Boy walks backward waving as Jade drags him along.

I think Walk's going to leave, too, but he stays at our table.

I grab my spoon back. "These are my friends, too."

"I got that."

"You got that?"

"I got that." He opens his milk carton top and closes it again. Open, close, open, close.

"It's not like it's been great at my house. My parents have been killing each other ever since my mom found out."

His eyes flash across me then look back down.

"Look, I don't get the whole problem here. I mean that Climpton guy was dead, anyway. Isn't it better to have a live dad than a dead one?"

His face seems to suck inside itself. He says nothing.

"Walk?"

He looks at me for the first time. He shakes his head like I am some kind of alien girl. "This isn't something you can understand," he says finally, working the milk carton again.

"Why?"

"It just isn't."

"I can't understand because I'm stupid . . . or because I'm white?"

"Look, I'm sure there are things I don't understand, either." Walk says this slowly like I am five.

"No you're not."

"Okay"—he shrugs—"I'm not."

"My father wants to be your dad, you know."

Walk snorts. "Your father got caught with his pants down. Now he's trying to recover."

"He's been watching you for, like, years. He goes to the Y to see you swim."

He stops moving the milk carton. He opens the top and pours the milk on the ground. "No he doesn't," he whispers.

"Yes," I say, "he does."

FIFTY-SIX

Walk

The moon has a chunk missing. It sits lopsided in the sky with black all around, dark as asphalt. The light from the carport shines on all the cars. Walk has a paper clip he's stretched to an almost straight line. He scoots down under the wheel well of Sylvia's car, takes the end of the paper clip, and scratches tiny letters in the brown unpainted edge.

I AM ME.

FIFTY-SEVEN

Kirsten

At school my mom turns into the drop-off. I dig for my backpack, which has slid under the seat.

"Hey," Kip says. "There's Walk in front of us!" She rolls down the window. "Hey, Walk! It's me, Kippy!" Kippy squeals like Walk is a rock star. She calls him every day now. I don't know what they talk about. I asked her once and she said, "Infinity."

Walk waves at Kippy. I hop out as my mother opens the door. She has one foot in, one foot out, her eyes intent on Sylvia.

A car pulls up behind us and honks. My mother jumps. Sylvia turns around.

My mother makes a fast motion with her hand. Was she swatting a fly or . . . ?

"Did you see that? Think my mom was *waving* at your mom?" I ask Walk.

"Yeah."

"Yeah?"

The warning bell rings. "C'mon, we're going to be late," Walk says.

"If we don't get our butts in gear." I huff after him.

"Always a butt involved with you," Walk calls over his shoulder.

"Gonna miss you when you leave," I say. "I'm not the only one, either."

"Guess I can't go, then."

I thunder after him, down the hall, up the stairs, and into class. I grab his arm as he sits down. "You're . . ."—I double over, out of breath—"kidding, right?"

He shrugs.

"You're staying?"

"Looks that way. Just do me a favor," he whispers. "Don't get weird about this."

"Okay, but . . . ," I whisper back, "how do I be normal about it?"

"Just go sit down, okay?"

"I can do that."

"All right, then?" He looks up at me. His dark brown eyes take me inside him. This is something important he's asking.

I nod. "This is good, Walk. You know. This whole thing."

"You're crazy," he whispers.

"No I'm not."

He bites his lip.

"You have to trust me," I say.

211

Kirsten

"Kirsten." His voice gets suddenly tight. He twists his pencil point into his binder, twists so hard it pops the lead right out. "Not all at once, okay?"

"Yeah," I tell him. "Okay."

Back in my seat I suddenly understand something I've never understood before. It matters who I am. I fit in the world. I do.

FIFTY-EIGHT

Walk

In Ms. Scrushy's class Brianna's elbow is back hangin' on his desk.

"Yes?" Walk asks.

"Just wanted to let you know I am so nice to Matteo's mother. So nice . . . you have no idea," she whispers.

"What's that supposed to mean?"

"It means I'm nice to her, okay? Ask Matteo. He'll tell you I've been good."

Walk watches her. "Yeah, so? What do you want, Brianna?"

Brianna shrugs. She runs her hand over his arm. "Hey, I don't want to make you mad."

He yanks his arm away. "Get off me."

"You love it and you know it."

Walk shakes his head. "You are so full of . . ." He knows he can't tell her what she's really full of.

"Hey." She beckons her finger like Walk should come close. "I want to ask you something."

Walk raises his eyebrows.

"Are you like half white?"

Walk's skin gets tight around him. He grinds his teeth. "No. I'm all white, can't you see?" Walk sticks out his arm. "This arm is all white. The other arm, Taiwanese. My left leg, Venezuelan. My right leg, from Portugal. I represent every ethnicity. Every religion, too, why not?"

"No, really," she whispers. "My mom said Kirsten's mom told some yoga friend who is Maya's mom's cousin that your dad is like Kirsten's dad."

"My dad likes Kirsten's dad?" Walk asks.

"No, he *is* Kirsten's dad."

"Wait, wait, wait. So my dad is Kirsten's dad? Who's your dad?"

"My dad is my dad," Brianna snips.

"Okay, okay. I have this straight now. Your dad is your dad. And my dad is Kirsten's dad. Phew"—Walk wipes his forehead—"thanks for figuring that out for me."

"So is it true or not?"

"Definitely true. Definitely," Walk tells her.

"Really?" she asks in her breathiest voice.

"Yes," Walk says. "And here's something you haven't heard." He beckons her close and whispers in her ear: "Matteo's dad is my mom."

She jerks away and takes her elbow back. "Shut up. Just shut up."

"Anytime you need to know somethin', just check with me, Brianna. Just check with me."

214

FIFTY-NINE

Kirsten

Kippy is sitting outside. We are both home with the flu, though she has a temperature and I don't. She has her new book, *The Gardener's Guide to Happy Trees*, on her lap and she is reading in a little chair.

The tree guy put some kind of poison on the stump to make it rot so it will be easier to dig out. Kippy cordoned off the stump and the new tree in its pot using an elaborate system of duct tape and bungee cords. She treats the whole area like a Native American burial ground.

"Come on," I tell her. "Mom's going to kill me for letting you sit out here. It's freezing."

"The tree should not still be in the planter," she tells me. "It says right here we could stunt its growth if we don't plant soon."

I shrug. "Maybe it will just be like a bonsai or something."

Kip rolls her eyes. "Does this look like a bonsai?"

"No."

"I'm tired of waiting," she tells me.

"Yeah, me, too. But you know what? It's been better lately. Mom's calmed way down. Dad's home more. They're gonna plant that tree, Kippy. I really think so."

SIXTY

Walk

Walker Jones
November 30
If a tree falls in the forest and no one hears it,
does it make a sound?

Yes.

Ms. Scrushy comes by and taps on Brianna's note-book. "At least two paragraphs," she reminds her. Walk keeps writing.

Sorry, Ms. Scrushy, but this question is pretty stupid. Trees don't change. They make the sounds they do whether anyone is out there hearing or not. But to say to a tree: "Hey, tree, you don't exist if no-body hears you . . ." That's just plain dumb.

A tree is a tree with all its sounds, sticks, leaves, dirt, roots, whatever. Anyone tells you otherwise, they're wrong.

Acknowledgments

I want to thank the kids at Charles Maclay Junior High (now Charles Maclay Middle School) in Pacoima, California, for teaching me what I needed to know in seventh grade so long ago. I'm especially grateful to Florence Vivian Hamilton, who never gave a whit what color I was.

I'd like to thank Stephanie Lee, Leah King, Wendy Pitts, Derek McDonald, and Alicia Bell for giving me their frank thoughts on drafts of this manuscript, and members of my Mill Valley Crit Group for their continual help and encouragement with this book.

I'd also like to express my deepest gratitude to my family—Jacob, Ian, and Kai—for giving me what I need every hour of every day.

—G. C.